PULP FICTION

PULP FICTION

a Quentin Tarantino screenplay

New York

PULP (pulp) n. 1. A soft, moist, shapeless mass of matter.

2. A magazine or book containing lurid subject matter and being characteristically printed on rough, unfinished paper.

—American Heritage Dictionary
New College Edition

Printed in the United States of America. For information address: Hyperion, 114 Fifth Avenue, New York, New York 10011.

Library of Congress Cataloging-in-Publication Data
Tarantino, Quentin.
Pulp fiction : a screenplay / by Quentin Tarantino.
p. cm.
ISBN: 0-7868-8104-6
1. Pulp fiction (Motion picture) I. Title.
PN1997.P86T37 1994
791.45'72—dc20 94-38752 CIP

First Edition

10 9 8 7

Foreword

Quentin Tarantino has hit the film world as hard as one of Sam Spade's uppercuts. Since his startling debut feature, *Reservoir Dogs,* in 1992 the former videostore clerk turned auteur has brilliantly finessed the divide between art-house cachet and commercial viability, and in the process become pointsman for an entire generation of filmmakers. *Pulp Fiction,* Tarantino's latest feature, merely confirms his promise as one of the most electrifying voices in film since the advent of Martin Scorsese. The story of an ensemble of couples, including a kingpin and his wife, a pair of killers-for-hire, and a down-on-his luck palooka, Tarantino's film takes its title from the cheap, groundwood magazines that emerged at the turn of the century and eventually made legends out of hardboiled types such as Dashiell Hammett and Raymond Chandler.

Tarantino's variant on the pulp legacy is tougher, fiercer, than many of the classic movies that were adapted from popular detective fiction—studio pictures like *The Maltese Falcon* and *Double Indemnity* where the gore was stanched and sex turned down to a simmer. At its looniest, *Pulp Fiction* reads like a demented hybrid of women's romance fiction and EC Comics, equal parts love idyll and splattertoon. Like his idol, Jean-Luc Godard, the young writer-director is a *pasticheur* and pop-cultural relativist, as content to riff on Elvis as Pam Grier and Shakespeare. Still, for all the allusions and insider banter, it would be a mistake to consider Tarantino as anything less than wholly his own invention.

Bone-shattering, skin-splitting, blood-spurting, Tarantino's cinema of viscera is written on the flesh of outlaw men and women, all of whom are far more complicated than their underworld types would suggest. In Tarantino's pulp fiction, the style is at once familiar and wild and fresh, while the concerns with violence, sexual identity, and, most provocatively of all, with race, are deeply, unmistakably contemporary. The hook in *Pulp Fiction* may be violence but the sinker is that here even God gets a chance. When Jules, Tarantino's killer who witnesses divine intervention, says, "I'm trying real hard to be a shepherd," it's a miracle that he's trying at all.

—*Manohla Dargis*

P U L P F I C T I O N

written & directed
by

Quentin Tarantino

stories
by

Quentin Tarantino
&
Roger Avary

THREE STORIES...

ABOUT ONE STORY...

May 1993
last draft

Blue: revised 8/18/93
Pink: revised 9/8/93
Green: revised 10/5/93

1. INT. COFFEE SHOP – MORNING 1.

A normal Denny's, Spires-like coffee shop in Los Angeles. It's about 9:00 in the morning. While the place isn't jammed, there's a healthy number of people drinking coffee, munching on bacon and eating eggs.

Two of these people are a YOUNG MAN and a YOUNG WOMAN. The Young Man has a slight working-class English accent and, like his fellow countrymen, smokes cigarettes like they're going out of style.

It is impossible to tell where the Young Woman is from or how old she is; everything she does contradicts something she did. The boy and girl sit in a booth. Their dialogue is to be said in a rapid-pace "HIS GIRL FRIDAY" fashion.

YOUNG MAN
No, forget it, it's too risky. I'm through doin' that shit.

YOUNG WOMAN
You always say that, the same thing every time: never again, I'm through, too dangerous.

YOUNG MAN
I know that's what I always say. I'm always right too, but --

YOUNG WOMAN
-- but you forget about it in a day or two --

YOUNG MAN
-- yeah, well, the days of me forgittin' are over, and the days of me rememberin' have just begun.

YOUNG WOMAN
When you go on like this, you know what you sound like?

YOUNG MAN
I sound like a sensible fucking man, is what I sound like.

YOUNG WOMAN
You sound like a duck.
(imitates a duck)
Quack, quack, quack, quack, quack, quack, quack....

YOUNG MAN
Well take heart, 'cause you're never gonna hafta hear it again. Because since I'm never gonna do it again, you're never gonna hafta hear me quack about how I'm never gonna do it again.

YOUNG WOMAN
After tonight.

The boy and girl laugh, their laughter putting a pause in their back and forth.

YOUNG MAN
(with a smile)
Correct. I got all tonight to quack.

A WAITRESS comes by with a pot of coffee.

WAITRESS
Can I get anybody any more coffee?

YOUNG WOMAN
Oh yes, thank you.

The Waitress pours the Young Woman's coffee. The Young Man lights up another cigarette.

YOUNG MAN
I'm doin' fine.

The Waitress leaves. The Young Man takes a drag off of his smoke. The Young Woman pours a ton of cream and sugar into her coffee.

The Young Man goes right back into it.

YOUNG MAN
I mean the way it is now, you're takin' the same fuckin' risk as when you rob a bank. You take more of a risk. Banks are easier! Federal banks aren't supposed to stop you anyway, during a robbery. They're insured, why should they care? You don't even need a gun in a federal bank.
(MORE)

YOUNG MAN (CONT'D)
I heard about this guy, walked into a federal bank with a portable phone, handed the phone to the teller, the guy on the other end of the phone said: "We got this guy's little girl, and if you don't give him all your money, we're gonna kill 'er."

YOUNG WOMAN
Did it work?

YOUNG MAN
Fuckin' A it worked, that's what I'm talkin' about! Knucklehead walks in a bank with a telephone, not a pistol, not a shotgun, but a fuckin' phone, cleans the place out, and they don't lift a fuckin' finger.

YOUNG WOMAN
Did they hurt the little girl?

YOUNG MAN
I don't know. There probably never was a little girl -- the point of the story isn't the little girl. The point of the story is they robbed the bank with a telephone.

YOUNG WOMAN
You wanna rob banks?

YOUNG MAN
I'm not sayin' I wanna rob banks, I'm just illustrating that if we did, it would be easier than what we been doin'.

YOUNG WOMAN
So you don't want to be a bank robber?

YOUNG MAN
Naw, all those guys are goin' down the same road, either dead or servin' twenty.

YOUNG WOMAN
And no more liquor stores?

YOUNG MAN

What have we been talking about? Yeah, no-more-liquor-stores. Besides, it ain't the giggle it usta be. Too many foreigners own liquor stores. Vietnamese, Koreans, they can't fuckin' speak English. You tell 'em: "Empty out the register," and they don't know what it fuckin' means. They make it too personal. We keep on, one of those gook motherfuckers gonna make us kill 'em.

YOUNG WOMAN

I'm not gonna kill anybody.

YOUNG MAN

I don't wanna kill anybody either. But they'll probably put us in a situation where it's us or them. And if it's not the gooks, it these old Jews who've owned the store for fifteen fuckin' generations. Ya got Grandpa Irving sittin' behind the counter with a fuckin' Magnum. Try walkin' into one of those stores with nothin' but a telephone, see how far it gets you. Fuck it, forget it, we're out of it.

YOUNG WOMAN

Well, what else is there, day jobs?

YOUNG MAN

(laughing)

Not this life.

YOUNG WOMAN

Well what then?

He calls to the Waitress.

YOUNG MAN

Garcon! Coffee!

Then looks to his girl.

YOUNG MAN

This place.

The Waitress comes by, pouring him some more.

WAITRESS
(snotty)
"Garcon" means boy.

She splits.

YOUNG WOMAN
Here? It's a coffee shop.

YOUNG MAN
What's wrong with that? People never rob restaurants, why not? Bars, liquor stores, gas stations, you get your head blown off stickin' up one of them. Restaurants, on the other hand, you catch with their pants down. They're not expecting to get robbed, or not as expecting.

YOUNG WOMAN
(taking to idea)
I bet in places like this you could cut down on the hero factor.

YOUNG MAN
Correct. Just like banks, these places are insured. The managers don't give a fuck, they're just tryin' to get ya out the door before you start pluggin' diners. Waitresses, forget it, they ain't takin' a bullet for the register. Busboys, some wetback gettin' paid a dollar fifty a hour gonna really give a fuck you're stealin' from the owner. Customers are sittin' there with food in their mouths, they don't know what's goin' on. One minute they're havin' a Denver omelette, next minute somebody's stickin' a gun in their face.

The Young Woman visibly takes in the idea. The Young Man continues in a low voice.

YOUNG MAN
See, I got the idea last liquor store we stuck up. 'Member all those customers kept comin' in?

YOUNG WOMAN
Yeah.

YOUNG MAN
Then you got the idea to take everybody's wallet.

YOUNG WOMAN
Uh-huh.

YOUNG MAN
That was a good idea.

YOUNG WOMAN
Thank you.

YOUNG MAN
We made more from the wallets than we did the register.

YOUNG WOMAN
Yes we did.

YOUNG MAN
A lot of people go to restaurants.

YOUNG WOMAN
A lot of wallets.

YOUNG MAN
Pretty smart, huh?

The Young Woman scans the restaurant with this new information. She sees all the PATRONS eating, lost in conversations. The tired WAITRESS, taking orders. The BUSBOYS going through the motions, collecting dishes. The MANAGER complaining to the COOK about something. A smiles breaks out on the Young Woman's face.

YOUNG WOMAN
Pretty smart.
(into it)
I'm ready, let's go, right here, right now.

YOUNG MAN
Remember, same as before, you're crowd control, I handle the employees.

YOUNG WOMAN
Got it.

They both take out their .32-caliber pistols and lay them on the table. He looks at her and she back at him.

YOUNG WOMAN
I love you, Pumpkin.

YOUNG MAN
I love you, Honey Bunny.

And with that, Pumpkin and Honey Bunny grab their weapons, stand up and rob the restaurant. Pumpkin's robbery persona is that of the in-control professional. Honey Bunny's is that of the psychopathic, hair-triggered, loose cannon.

PUMPKIN
(yelling to all)
Everybody be cool, this is a robbery!

HONEY BUNNY
Any of you fuckin' pricks move and I'll execute every one of you motherfuckers! Got that?

CUT TO:

CREDIT SEQUENCE:

PULP FICTION

2. INT. '74 CHEVY (MOVING) – MORNING 2.

An old gas guzzling, dirty, white 1974 Chevy Nova BARRELS down a homeless-ridden street in Hollywood. In the front seat are two young fellas -- one white, one black -- both wearing cheap black suits with thin black ties under long green dusters. Their names are VINCENT VEGA (white) and JULES WINNFIELD (black). Jules is behind the wheel.

JULES
-- okay now, tell me about the hash bars?

VINCENT
What do you want to know?

JULES
Well, hash is legal there, right?

VINCENT
Yeah, it's legal, but it ain't a hundred percent legal. I mean you can't walk into a restaurant, roll a joint, and start puffin' away.
(MORE)

VINCENT (CONT'D)
You're only supposed to smoke in your home or certain designated places.

JULES
Those are hash bars?

VINCENT
Yeah, it breaks down like this: it's legal to buy it, it's legal to own it and, if you're the proprietor of a hash bar, it's legal to sell it. It's legal to carry it, which doesn't really matter 'cause -- get a load of this -- if the cops stop you, it's illegal for them to search you. Searching you is a right that the cops in Amsterdam don't have.

JULES
That did it, man -- I'm fuckin' goin', that's all there is to it.

VINCENT
You'll dig it the most. But you know what the funniest thing about Europe is?

JULES
What?

VINCENT
It's the little differences. A lotta the same shit we got here, they got there, but there they're a little different.

JULES
Example?

VINCENT
Well, in Amsterdam, you can buy beer in a movie theater. And I don't mean in a paper cup either. They give you a glass of beer, like in a bar. In Paris, you can buy beer at McDonald's. Also, you know what they call a Quarter Pounder with Cheese in Paris?

JULES
They don't call it a Quarter Pounder with Cheese?

VINCENT
No, they got the metric system there, they wouldn't know what the fuck a Quarter Pounder is.

JULES
What'd they call it?

VINCENT
Royale with Cheese.

JULES
(repeating)
Royale with Cheese. What'd they call a Big Mac?

VINCENT
Big Mac's a Big Mac, but they call it Le Big Mac.

JULES
What do they call a Whopper?

VINCENT
I dunno, I didn't go into a Burger King. But you know what they put on french fries in Holland instead of ketchup?

JULES
What?

VINCENT
Mayonnaise.

JULES
Goddamn!

VINCENT
I seen 'em do it. And I don't mean a little bit on the side of the plate, they fuckin' drown 'em in it.

JULES
Uuccch!

CUT TO:

3. INT. CHEVY (TRUNK) — MORNING 3.

The trunk of the Chevy OPENS UP, Jules and Vincent reach inside, taking out two .45 Automatics, loading and cocking them.

JULES
We should have shotguns for this kind of deal.

VINCENT
How many up there?

JULES
Three or four.

VINCENT
Counting our guy?

JULES
I'm not sure.

VINCENT
So there could be five guys up there?

JULES
It's possible.

VINCENT
We should have fuckin' shotguns.

They CLOSE the trunk.

CUT TO:

4. EXT. APARTMENT BUILDING COURTYARD — MORNING 4.

Vincent and Jules, their long matching overcoats practically dragging on the ground, walk through the courtyard of what looks like a hacienda-style Hollywood apartment building.

We TRACK alongside.

VINCENT
What's her name?

JULES
Mia.

VINCENT
How did Marsellus and her meet?

JULES
I dunno, however people meet people. She usta be an actress.

VINCENT
She ever do anything I woulda saw?

JULES
I think her biggest deal was she starred in a pilot.

VINCENT
What's a pilot?

JULES
Well, you know the shows on TV?

VINCENT
I don't watch TV.

JULES
Yes, but you're aware that there's an invention called television, and on that invention they show shows?

VINCENT
Yeah.

JULES
Well, the way they pick the shows on TV is they make one show, and that show's called a pilot. And they show that one show to the people who pick the shows, and on the strength of that one show, they decide if they want to make more shows. Some get accepted and become TV programs, and some don't, and become nothing. She starred in one of the ones that became nothing.

They enter the apartment building.

5. INT. RECEPTION AREA (APARTMENT BUILDING) – MORNING 5.

Vincent and Jules walk through the reception area and wait for the elevator.

JULES
You remember Antwan Rockamora? Half-black, half-Samoan, usta call him Tony Rocky Horror.

VINCENT
Yeah maybe, fat right?

JULES
I wouldn't go so far as to call the brother fat. He's got a weight problem. What's the nigger gonna do, he's Samoan.

VINCENT
I think I know who you mean, what about him?

JULES
Well, Marsellus fucked his ass up good. And word around the campfire, it was on account of Marsellus Wallace's wife.

The elevator arrives, the men step inside.

6. INT. ELEVATOR – MORNING 6.

VINCENT
What'd he do, fuck her?

JULES
No no no no no no no, nothin' that bad.

VINCENT
Well what then?

JULES
He gave her a foot massage.

VINCENT
A foot massage?

Jules nods his head: "Yes."

VINCENT
That's all?

Jules nods his head: "Yes."

VINCENT
What did Marsellus do?

JULES
Sent a couple of guys over to his place. They took him out on the patio of his apartment, threw his ass over the balcony. Nigger fell four stories. They had this garden at the bottom, enclosed in glass, like one of them greenhouses -- nigger fell through that. Since then, he's kinda developed a speech impediment.

The elevator doors open, Jules and Vincent exit.

VINCENT
That's a damn shame.

7. INT. APARTMENT BUILDING HALLWAY – MORNING 7.

STEADICAM in front of Jules and Vincent as they make a beeline down the hall.

VINCENT
Still I hafta say, play with matches, ya get burned.

JULES
Whaddya mean?

VINCENT
You don't be givin' Marsellus Wallace's new bride a foot massage.

JULES
You don't think he overreacted?

VINCENT
Antwan probably didn't expect Marsellus to react like he did, but he had to expect a reaction.

JULES
It was a foot massage, a foot massage is nothing, I give my mother a foot massage.

VINCENT
It's laying hands on Marsellus Wallace's new wife in a familiar way. Is it as bad as eatin' her out -- no, but you're in the same fuckin' ballpark.

Jules stops Vincent.

JULES
Whoa...whoa...whoa...stop right there. Eatin' a bitch out, and givin' a bitch a foot massage ain't even the same fuckin' thing.

VINCENT
Not the same thing, the same ballpark.

JULES
It ain't no ballpark either. Look maybe your method of massage differs from mine, but touchin' his lady's feet, and stickin' your tongue in her holyiest of holyies, ain't the same ballpark, ain't the same league, ain't even the same fuckin' sport. Foot massages don't mean shit.

VINCENT
Have you ever given a foot massage?

JULES
Don't be tellin' me about foot massages -- I'm the fuckin' foot master.

VINCENT
Given a lot of 'em?

JULES
Shit yeah. I got my technique down man, I don't tickle or nothin'.

VINCENT
Have you ever given a guy a foot massage?

Jules looks at him a long moment -- he's been set up.

JULES
Fuck you.

He starts walking down the hall. Vincent, smiling, walks a little bit behind.

VINCENT
How many?

JULES
Fuck you.

VINCENT
Would you give me a foot massage -- I'm kinda tired.

JULES
Man, you best back off, I'm gittin' pissed -- this is the door.

The two men stand in front of a door numbered "49." They whisper.

JULES
What time is it?

VINCENT
(checking his watch)
Seven-twenty-two in the morning.

JULES
It ain't quite time, let's hang back.

They move a little away from the door, facing each other, still whispering.

JULES
Look, just because I wouldn't give no man a foot massage, don't make it right for Marsellus to throw Antwan off a building into a glass-motherfuckin-house, fuckin' up the way the nigger talks. That ain't right, man. Motherfucker do that to me, he better paralyze my ass, 'cause I'd kill'a motherfucker.

VINCENT
I'm not sayin' he was right, but you're sayin' a foot massage don't mean nothin', and I'm sayin' it does. I've given a million ladies a million foot massages and they all meant somethin'. We act like they don't, but they do. That's what's so fuckin' cool about 'em.
(MORE)

VINCENT (CONT'D)
This sensual thing's goin' on that nobody's talkin about, but you know it and she knows it, fuckin' Marsellus knew it, and Antwan shoulda known fuckin' better. That's his fuckin' wife, man. He ain't gonna have a sense of humor about that shit.

JULES
That's an interesting point, but let's get into character.

VINCENT
What's her name again?

JULES
Mia. Why you so interested in big man's wife?

VINCENT
Well, Marsellus is leavin' for Florida and when he's gone, he wants me to take care of Mia.

JULES
Take care of her?

Making a gun out of his finger and placing it to his head.

VINCENT
Not that! Take her out. Show her a good time. Don't let her get lonely.

JULES
You're gonna be takin' Mia Wallace out on a date?

VINCENT
It ain't a date. It's like when you and your buddy's wife go to a movie or somethin'. It's just... you know...good company.

Jules just looks at him.

VINCENT
It's not a date.

Jules just looks at him.

VINCENT
I'm not gonna be a bad boy.

Jules shakes his head and mumbles to himself.

JULES
Bitch gonna kill more niggers than time.

VINCENT
What was that?

JULES
Nothin'. Let's get into character.

VINCENT
What'd you say?

JULES
I didn't say shit. Let's go to work.

VINCENT
Don't play with me, you said somethin', now what was it?

JULES
(referring to the job)
Do you wanna do this?

VINCENT
I want you to repeat what you said.

JULES
That door's gonna open in about thirty seconds, so git yourself together --

VINCENT
-- my self is together --

JULES
-- bullshit it is. Stop thinkin' 'bout that Ho, and get yourself together like a qualified pro.

8. INT. APARTMENT (ROOM 49) – MORNING 8.

THREE YOUNG GUYS, obviously in over their heads, sit at a table with hamburgers, french fries and soda pops laid out.

One of them flips the LOUD BOLT on the door, opening it to REVEAL Jules and Vincent in the hallway.

JULES
Hey kids.

The two men stroll inside.

The three young caught-off-guard Guys are:

MARVIN
The black young man, who opened the door, will, as the scene progresses, back into the corner.

ROGER
A young blond-haired surfer kid with a "Flock of Seagulls" haircut, who has yet to say a word, sits at the table with a big sloppy hamburger in his hand.

BRETT
A white, preppy-looking sort with a blow-dry haircut.

Vincent and Jules take in the place, with their hands in their pockets. Jules is the one who does the talking.

JULES
How you boys doin'?

No answer.

JULES
(to Brett)
Am I trippin', or did I just ask you a question?

BRETT
We're doin' okay.

As Jules and Brett talk, Vincent moves behind the young Guys.

JULES
Do you know who we are?

Brett shakes his head: "No."

JULES
We're associates of your business partner Marsellus Wallace, you remember your business partner dont'ya?

No answer.

JULES
(to Brett)
Now I'm gonna take a wild guess here: you're Brett, right?

BRETT
I'm Brett.

JULES
I thought so. Well, you remember your business partner Marsellus Wallace, dont'ya Brett?

BRETT
I remember him.

JULES
Good for you. Looks like me and Vincent caught you at breakfast, sorry 'bout that. What'cha eatin'?

BRETT
Hamburgers.

JULES
Hamburgers. The cornerstone of any nutritious breakfast. What kinda hamburgers?

BRETT
Cheeseburgers.

JULES
No, I mean where did you get'em? McDonald's, Wendy's, Jack-in-the-Box, where?

BRETT
Big Kahuna Burger.

JULES
Big Kahuna Burger. That's that Hawaiian burger joint. I heard they got some tasty burgers. I ain't never had one myself, how are they?

BRETT
They're good.

JULES
Mind if I try one of yours?

BRETT

No.

JULES

Yours is this one, right?

BRETT

Yeah.

Jules grabs the burger and takes a bite of it.

JULES

Uuummmm, that's a tasty burger.
(to Vincent)
Vince, you ever try a Big Kahuna Burger?

VINCENT

No.

Jules holds out the Big Kahuna.

JULES

You wanna bite, they're real good.

VINCENT

I ain't hungry.

JULES

Well, if you like hamburgers give 'em a try sometime. Me, I can't usually eat 'em 'cause my girlfriend's a vegetarian. Which more or less makes me a vegetarian, but I sure love the taste of a good burger.
(to Brett)
You know what they call a Quarter Pounder with Cheese in France?

BRETT

No.

JULES

Tell 'em, Vincent.

VINCENT

Royale with Cheese.

JULES

Royale with Cheese, you know why they call it that?

BRETT
Because of the metric system?

JULES
Check out the big brain on Brett. You'a smart motherfucker, that's right. The metric system.
(he points at a fast food drink cup)
What's in this?

BRETT
Sprite.

JULES
Sprite, good, mind if I have some of your tasty beverage to wash this down with?

BRETT
Sure.

Jules grabs the cup and takes a sip.

JULES
Uuuuummmm, hits the spot!
(to Roger)
You, Flock of Seagulls, you know what we're here for?

Roger nods his head: "Yes."

JULES
Then why don't you tell my boy here Vince, where you got the shit hid.

MARVIN
It's under the be --

JULES
-- I don't remember askin' you a goddamn thing.
(to Roger)
You were sayin'?

ROGER
It's under the bed.

Vincent moves to the bed, reaches underneath it, pulling out a black snap briefcase.

VINCENT
Got it.

Vincent flips the two locks, opening the case. We can't see what's inside, but a small glow emits from the case. Vincent just stares at it, transfixed.

JULES
We happy?

No answer from the transfixed Vincent.

JULES
Vincent!

Vincent looks up at Jules.

JULES
We happy?

Closing the case.

VINCENT
We're happy.

BRETT
(to Jules)
Look, what's your name? I got his name's Vincent, but what's yours?

JULES
My name's Pitt, and you ain't talkin' your ass outta this shit.

BRETT
I just want you to know how sorry we are about how fucked up things got between us and Mr. Wallace. When we entered into this thing, we only had the best intentions --

As Brett talks, Jules takes out his gun and SHOOTS Roger three times in the chest, BLOWING him out of his chair.

Vince smiles to himself. Jules has got style.

Brett has just shit his pants. He's not crying or whimpering, but he's so full of fear, it's as if his body is imploding.

JULES
(to Brett)
Oh, I'm sorry. Did that break your concentration? I didn't mean to do that. Please, continue. I believe you were saying something about "best intentions."

Brett can't say a word.

JULES
Whatsamatter? Oh, you were through anyway. Well, let me retort. Would you describe for me what Marsellus Wallace looks like?

Brett still can't speak.

Jules SNAPS, SAVAGELY TIPPING the card table over, removing the only barrier between himself and Brett. Brett now sits in a lone chair before Jules like a political prisoner in front of an interrogator.

JULES
What country you from!

BRETT
(petrified)
What?

JULES
"What" ain't no country I know! Do they speak English in "What?"

BRETT
(near heart attack)
What?

JULES
English-motherfucker-can-you-speak-it?

BRETT
Yes.

JULES
Then you understand what I'm sayin'?

BRETT
Yes.

JULES
Now describe what Marsellus Wallace looks like!

BRETT
(out of fear)
What?

Jules takes his .45 and PRESSES the barrel HARD in Brett's cheek.

JULES
Say "What" again! C'mon, say "What" again! I dare ya, I double dare ya motherfucker, say "What" one more goddamn time!

Brett is regressing on the spot.

JULES
Now describe to me what Marsellus Wallace looks like!

Brett does his best.

BRETT
Well he's...he's...black --

JULES
-- go on!

BRETT
...and he's...he's...tall --

JULES
-- does he look like a bitch?!

BRETT
(without thinking)
What?

Jules' eyes go to Vincent, Vincent smirks, Jules rolls his eyes and SHOOTS Brett in the shoulder.

Brett SCREAMS, breaking into a SHAKING/TREMBLING SPASM in the chair.

JULES
Does-he-look-like-a-bitch?!

BRETT
(in agony)
No.

JULES
Then why did you try to fuck 'im like a bitch?!

BRETT
(in spasm)
I didn't.

Now in a lower voice.

JULES
Yes ya did Brett. Ya tried ta fuck 'im. You ever read the Bible, Brett?

BRETT
(in spasm)
Yes.

JULES
There's a passage I got memorized, seems appropriate for this situation: Ezekiel 25:17. "The path of the righteous man is beset on all sides by the inequities of the selfish and the tyranny of evil men. Blessed is he who, in the name of charity and good will, shepherds the weak through the valley of darkness, for he is truly his brother's keeper and the finder of lost children. And I will strike down upon thee with great vengeance and furious anger those who attempt to poison and destroy my brothers. And you will know my name is the Lord when I lay my vengeance upon you."

The two men EMPTY their guns at the same time on the sitting Brett.

When they are finished, the bullet-ridden carcass just sits there for a moment, then TOPPLES over.

All is quiet.

The only SOUND is Marvin MUTTERING in the corner.

MARVIN
...goddamn...goddamn...that was fucked up...goddamn, that was cold-blooded....

VINCENT
(pointing to Marvin)
Friend of yours?

JULES
Yeah, Marvin-Vincent-Vincent-Marvin.

VINCENT

Tell 'em to shut up, he's gettin' on my nerves.

JULES

Marvin, I'd knock that shit off if I was you.

Then suddenly the bathroom door BURSTS OPEN, and a FOURTH MAN (as young as the rest) comes CHARGING out, a silver Magnum in his hand.

We DOLLY into a MEDIUM on him.

FOURTH MAN

Die...die...die...die...die...die!

The Fourth Man FIRES SIX BOOMING SHOTS from his hand cannon in the direction of Vincent and Jules. He SCREAMS a maniacal cry of revenge until he's DRY FIRING.

Then...his face does a complete change of expression. It goes from a "Vengeance is mine" expression, to a "What the fuck" blank look.

FOURTH MAN

I don't understand --

The Fourth Man is BLOWN OFF HIS FEET and OUT OF FRAME by bullets that TEAR HIM TO SHREDS.

He leaves the FRAME EMPTY.

FADE TO BLACK

Against black, TITLE CARD:

"VINCENT VEGA
AND
MARSELLUS WALLACE'S WIFE"

FADE IN:

9. MEDIUM SHOT – BUTCH COOLIDGE 9.

we FADE UP on Butch Coolidge, a white, 26-year old prizefighter. Butch sits at a table wearing a red and blue high school athletic jacket. Talking to him OFF SCREEN is everybody's boss MARSELLUS WALLACE. The black man sounds like a cross between a gangster and a king.

MARSELLUS

I think you're gonna find -- when all this shit is over and done -- I think you're gonna find yourself one smilin' motherfucker. Thing is Butch, right now you got ability. But your days are about over. See, painful as it may be, ability don't last. Now that's a hard motherfuckin' fact of life, but it's a fact of life your ass is gonna hafta git realistic about. This business is filled to the brim with unrealistic motherfuckers who thought their ass aged like wine. If you mean it turns to vinegar, it does. If you mean it gets better with age, it don't. Besides, how many fights you think you got left? Two? Boxers don't have old timers day. You came close, but you never made it. And if you were gonna make it, you'd a made it before now.

A hand lays an envelope full of money on the table in front of Butch. Butch picks it up.

Now, the night of the fight, you may feel a slight sting, that's pride fuckin' wit ya'. Fuck pride! Pride only hurts, it never helps. Fight through that shit. Cause a year from now when you're kickin' it in the Caribbean you're gonna say, Marsellus Wallace was right.

BUTCH

I got no problems with that.

MARSELLUS (OS)

In the fifth, your ass goes down.

Butch nods his head: "yes."

MARSELLUS (OS)

Say it!

BUTCH

In the fifth, my ass goes down.

CUT TO:

10. INT. CAR (MOVING) – DAY 10.

Vincent Vega looks really cool behind the wheel of a 1964 cherry-red Chevy Malibu convertible. From the car radio, ROCKABILLY MUSIC PLAYS. The b.g. is a COLORFUL PROCESS SHOT

11. EXT. SALLY LeROY'S – DAY 11.

Sally LeRoy's is a large topless bar by LAX that Marsellus owns.

Vincent's classic Malibu WHIPS into the near empty parking lot and parks next to a white Honda Civic.

Vince knocks on the door. The front entrance is unlocked, revealing the Dapper Dan fellow on the inside: ENGLISH DAVE. Dave isn't really English, he's a young black man from Baldwin Park, who has run a few clubs for Marsellus, including Sally LeRoy's.

ENGLISH DAVE
Vincent Vega, our man in Amsterdam, git your ass on in here.

Vincent, carrying the black briefcase from the scene between Vincent and Jules, steps inside. English Dave SLAMS the door in our faces.

12. INT. SALLY LeROY'S – DAY 12.

The spacious club is empty this time of day. English Dave crosses to the bar, and Vince follows.

VINCENT
Where's big man?

ENGLISH DAVE
He's over there, finishing up some business.

VINCENT'S POV:
Butch shakes hands with a huge figure with his back to us. The huge figure is the infamous and as of yet still UNSEEN Marsellus.

ENGLISH DAVE (OS)
Hang back for a second or two, and when you see the white boy leave, go on over. In the meanwhile, can I make you an espresso?

VINCENT
How 'bout a cup of just plain ol' American?

ENGLISH DAVE
Comin' up. I hear you're taking Mia out tomorrow?

VINCENT
At Marsellus' request.

ENGLISH DAVE
Have you met Mia?

VINCENT
Not yet.

English Dave smiles to himself.

VINCENT
What's so funny?

ENGLISH DAVE
Not a goddamn thing.

VINCENT
Look, I'm not an idiot. She's the big man's fuckin' wife. I'm gonna sit across a table, chew my food with my mouth closed, laugh at her jokes and that's all I'm gonna do.

English Dave puts Vince's coffee in front of him.

ENGLISH DAVE
My name's Paul, and this is between y'all.

Butch bellies up to the bar next to Vincent, drinking his cup of "plain ol' American."

BUTCH
(to English Dave)
Can I get a pack'a Red Apples?

ENGLISH DAVE
Filters?

BUTCH
Non.

While Butch waits for his smokes, Vincent just sips his coffee, staring at him. Butch looks over at him.

BUTCH
Lookin' at somethin', friend?

VINCENT
I ain't your friend, palooka.

Butch does a slow burn toward Vincent.

BUTCH
What was that?

VINCENT
I think ya heard me just fine, punchy.

Butch turns his body to Vincent, when....

MARSELLUS (OS)
Vincent Vega has entered the building, git your ass over here!

Vincent walks forward OUT OF FRAME, never giving Butch another glance. We DOLLY INTO CU on Butch, left alone in the FRAME, looking like he's ready to go into the manners-teaching business.

BUTCH'S POV:
Vincent hugging and kissing the obscured figure that is Marsellus.

Butch makes the wise decision that if this asshole's a friend of Marsellus, he better let it go -- for now.

ENGLISH DAVE (OS)
Pack of Red Apples, dollar-forty.

Butch is snapped out of his ass-kicking thoughts. He pays English Dave and walks out of the SHOT.

DISSOLVE TO:

13. INT. LANCE'S HOUSE (KITCHEN) — NIGHT 13.

CU JODY
a woman who appears to have a fondness for earrings. Both of her ears are pierced five times. She also sports rings in her lip, eyebrows and nose.

JODY
...I'll lend it to you. It's a great book on body-piercing.

Jody, Vincent and a young woman named TRUDI sit at the kitchen table of a suburban house in Echo Park. Even though Vince is at the same table, he's not included in the conversation.

TRUDI
You know how they use that gun when they pierce your ears? They don't use that when they pierce your nipples, do they?

JODY
Forget that gun. That gun goes against the entire idea behind piercing. All of my piercing, sixteen places on my body, every one of 'em done with a needle. Five in each ear. One through the nipple of my left breast. One through my right nostril. One through my left eyebrow. One through my lip. One in my clit. And I wear a stud in my tongue.

Vince has been letting this conversation go through one ear and out the other, until that last remark.

VINCENT
(interrupting)
Excuse me, sorry to interrupt. I'm curious, why would you get a stud in your tongue?

Jody looks at him and says as if it were the most obvious thing in the world.

JODY
It's a sex thing. It helps fellatio.

That thought never occurred to Vincent, but he can't deny it makes sense. Jody continues talking to Trudi, leaving Vincent to ponder the truth of her statement.

LANCE (OS)
Vince, you can come in now!

14. INT. LANCE'S BEDROOM – NIGHT 14.

Lance, late-20s, is a young man with a wild and woolly appearance that goes hand-in-hand with his wild and woolly personality. Lance has been selling drugs his entire adult life. He's never had a day job, never filed a tax return and has never been arrested. He wears a red flannel shirt over a "Speed Racer" tee-shirt.

Three bags of heroin lie on Lance's bed.

Lance and Vincent stand at the foot of the bed.

LANCE

Now this is Panda, from Mexico. Very good stuff. This is Bava, different, but equally good. And this is Choco from the Hartz Mountains of Germany. Now the first two are the same, forty-five an ounce -- those are friend prices -- but this one...

(pointing to the Choco)

...this one's a little more expensive. It's fifty-five. But when you shoot it, you'll know where that extra money went. Nothing wrong with the first two. It's real, real, real, good shit. But this one's a fuckin' madman.

VINCENT

Remember, I just got back from Amsterdam.

LANCE

Am I a nigger? Are you in Inglewood? No. You're in my house. White people who know the difference between good shit and bad shit, this is the house they come to. My shit, I'll take the Pepsi Challenge with Amsterdam shit any ol' day of the fuckin' week.

VINCENT

That's a bold statement.

LANCE

This ain't Amsterdam, Vince. This is a seller's market. Coke is fuckin' dead as disco. Heroin's comin' back in a big fuckin' way. It's this whole seventies retro. Bell bottoms, heroin, they're as hot as hell.

Vincent takes out a roll of money that would choke a horse to death.

VINCENT

Give me three hundred worth of the madman. If it's as good as you say, I'll be back for a thousand.

LANCE
I just hope I still have it. Whaddya think of Trudi? She ain't got a boyfriend, wanna hang out an' get high?

VINCENT
Which one's Trudi? The one with all the shit in her face?

LANCE
No, that's Jody. That's my wife.

Vincent and Lance giggle at the "faux pas."

VINCENT
I'm on my way somewhere. I got a dinner engagement. Rain check?

LANCE
No problemo.

Vincent takes out his case of works (utensils for shooting up).

VINCENT
You don't mind if I shoot up here?

LANCE
Mi casa, su casa.

VINCENT
Muchas gracias.

Vincent takes his works out of his case and, as the two continue to talk, Vince shoots up.

LANCE
Still got your Malibu?

VINCENT
You know what some fucker did to it the other day?

LANCE
What?

VINCENT
Fuckin' keyed it.

LANCE
Oh man, that's fucked up.

VINCENT

Tell me about it. I had the goddam thing in storage three years. It's out five days -- five days, and some dickless peace of shit fucks with it.

LANCE

They should be fuckin killed. No trial, no jury, straight to execution.

As he cooks his heroin.

VINCENT

I just wish I caught em doing it, ya know? Oh man, I'd give anything to catch em doing it. It'a been worth him doing it, if I coulda just caught em, you know what I mean?

LANCE

Well, it's like last week I go to Panorama City. Now when I go to Panorama City, I might as well be going to fuckin Nebraska, I'm about as familiar with both of em. I mean I never go down there. But anyway, last week I gotta go. So I go down there, and guess what? I get lost. So I pull into a gas station, now remember, bout a hundred years ago, when you usta get lost, you'd pull in a gas station ask the guy directions? Well stupid me, I'm still suffering from the delusion that you can still do that. So I ask the guy directions. He gives em to me, but there's somethin funny bout him em, I don't think to much about it, maybe he's just funny, but I notice it. So I drive off. I got so fuckin lost. When I finally break down and call the place, I find out I'm twenty fuckin miles in the wrong direction.

(MORE)

LANCE (CONT'D)
The only thing I can figure out is the dick bait at the gas station gave me the wrong directions on purpose. What a fucker! A fellow American comes up to you asking for help, and you purposely fuck him up. What kind of a world do we live in where people give people the wrong directions on purpose?

VINCENT
It's chicken shit. What's more chicken shit than fuckin with a guy's automobile? You don't fuck another man's vehicle. That's against the rules, you don't do that.

CU THE NEEDLE
going into Vincent's vein.

CU BLOOD
shooting into casing, mixing with the heroin.

CU OF VINCENT'S THUMB
push down on the plunger.

CUT TO:

15. EXT. MARSELLUS WALLACE'S HOUSE – NIGHT 15.

Vincent walks up to the driveway leading to Marsellus Wallace's front door. When he gets to the door, he hears MUSIC on the other side, and a note in plain view taped to it. He rips it off.

CU – NOTE

"Hi Vincent,
I'm getting dressed. The door's open. Come inside and make yourself a drink.
Mia"

Vincent neatly folds the note up, sticks it in his pocket, takes a here-goes-nothing breath and turns the knob.

16. INT. MARSELLUS WALLACE'S HOUSE – NIGHT 16.

As Vincent steps inside, the MUSIC that was behind the door, SWELLS drastically. Vincent, hands in pockets, strolls inside, checking out his boss' home.

VINCENT
(yelling)
Hello! I'm here!

We hear a DOOR OPEN, Vincent turns in its direction.

17. INT. DRESSING ROOM – NIGHT 17.

We're inside the room where the MUSIC is PLAYING. In the f.g. MIA WALLACE, naked with her back to us, talks to Vincent through a crack in the door. The door shields the front of her body from Vincent.

MIA
Vincent Vega?

VINCENT
I'm Vincent, you Mia?

MIA
That's me, pleased to meetcha. I'm still getting dressed. To your left, past the kitchen, is a bar. Why don't you make yourself a drink, have a seat in the living room, and I'll be out within three shakes of a lamb's tail.

VINCENT
Take your time.

Mia closes the door. Before she can fully turn around and show us her face....

WE CUT:

BACK TO VINCENT
standing where he was, MUSIC beating, looking at the closed door. We slowly ZOOM to the door.

We slowly ZOOM from a MEDIUM SHOT to CU on Vincent as he contemplates what's on the other side of the door. When we reach a CU, he walks OUT OF FRAME, breaking the spell.

Vincent walks to the bar and pours himself a drink.

WE JUXTAPOSE
as the MUSIC plays.

Mia's dress selection is taken out of the closet.

Vincent, drink in hand, moves into the living room.

Mia, her back to CAMERA, dressed in her pretty dress, checks herself in the mirror. We DOLLY towards her. Her face is still obscured.

CU — PORTRAIT OF MIA
hanging on the living room wall, showing Mia sensually reclining on a couch.

HIGH ANGLE SHOT OF VINCENT
looking up at the portrait.

CU — Mia cutting a huge line of coke on her vanity table with a credit card.

Vincent sits on a plush, comfy couch.

CU — MIA'S NOSE
snorting the line from a rolled up dollar bill.

Vincent on the couch, drink in hand. The SONG abruptly CUTS OFF.

CU — CD PLAYER OPENING
Mia's hand comes in and takes the CD out.

The CAMERA follows behind Mia's bare feet as she walks out of the dressing room, through the dining room, through the kitchen and into the living room.

SHOT THROUGH A VIDEO CAMERA
Mia has a camcorder and is videotaping Vincent on the couch. He looks up and sees her.

MIA (OS)
Smile, you're on Mia's camera!

VINCENT
Ready to go?

MIA (OS)
* Not yet, we're makin a movie. Let *
* me get into position. *

*MIA/CAMERA moves over by the coffee table, plopping *
*down on the floor. Vincent is now framed in a LOW *
*ANGLE MEDIUM SHOT. *

* MIA (OS) *
* Did ya ever watch Barbara Walters *
* interview the movie stars? *

* VINCENT *
* Once or twice. *

* MIA (OS) *
* Well that's what this is, pretend *
* I'm Barbara Walters. Now I'm gonna *
* ask you a bunch of questions-- *

* VINCENT *
* --About what? *

* MIA (OS) *
* Yourself....the world....life.... *
* god....whatever I feel would be *
* interesting. *

* VINCENT *
* I don't like answering questions. *

* MIA (OS) *
* That's not your problem. I'm the *
* interviewer, it's my problem. I have *
* to make you comfortable, so you'll *
* open up and reveal things you *
* normally wouldn't. We'll start with *
* a easy one. What's your name. *

* VINCENT *
* Vincent Vega *

* MIA (OS) *
* Any relation to Suzanne Vega? *

VINCENT
Yeah, she's my cousin.

MIA (OS)
Suzanne Vega the folk singer is your cousin?

VINCENT

Suzanne Vega's my cousin. If she's become a folk singer, I sure as hell don't know nothin about it. But then I haven't been to too many Thanksgivings lately.

MIA (OS)

Now I'm gonna ask you a bunch of quick questions I've come up, with, that more or less tell me what kind of person I'm having dinner with. My theory is that when it comes to important subjects, there's only two ways a person can answer. And which way they choose, tells you who that person is. For instance, there's two kind of people in this world, Elvis people and Beatles people. Now Beatles people, can like Elvis. And Elvis people, can like the Beatles. But nobody, likes them both equally. Somewhere you have to make a choice. And that choice, tells you who you are. Now I don't need to ask you that one, cause your obviously a Elvis person. But your hip to where I'm comin from? Can ya dig it?

VINCENT

I can dig it.

MIA (OS)

I knew you could. First question, Brady Bunch or The Partridge Family?

VINCENT

The Partridge Family all the way.

MIA (OS)

On "Rich Man, Poor Man", who did you like; Peter Strauss or Nick Nolte?

VINCENT

Nick Nolte, of course.

MIA (OS)

Are you a "Bewitched" man or a "Jeannie" man?

VINCENT
"Bewitched" all the way, though I always dug how Jeannie always called Larry Hagman master.

MIA (OS)
Staying on the "Bewitched" theme, who was the best Darren?

*Vincent looks at her like this is the most obvious
*answer in the world.

VINCENT
Do I even need to say the words?

MIA (OS)
No, but I had to ask, you understand?

VINCENT
Sure.

MIA (OS)
What's your favorite way to say "Thanks" in another language?

VINCENT
Merci beau coup.

MIA (OS)
In conversations, do you listen, or wait to talk?

VINCENT
I hafta admit I wait to talk, but I'm trying harder to listen.

MIA (OS)
If you were "Archie", who would you fuck first, Betty or Veronica?

VINCENT
Betty, I never understood Veronica's attraction.

MIA (OS)
Have you ever fantasised about being beaten up by a girl?

VINCENT
Sure.

MIA (OS)
Who?

VINCENT
Emma Peel on "The Avengers". That tough girl who usta hang out with Encyclopedia Brown. And Arlene Motika.

MIA (OS)
Who's Arlene Motika?

VINCENT
Girl from sixth grade, you don't know her.

CU – MIA
lowers the camcorder from in front of her face, and we get our first full on look at her. When we do we get a pretty good idea why Marsellus feels the way he does. She breaks out a blinding smile.

MIA
Cut. Print. Let's go eat.

18. EXT – JACKRABBIT SLIM'S – NIGHT 18.

In the past six years, fifties diners have sprung up all over LA, giving Thai restaurants a run for their money. They're all basically the same. Decor out of a "Archie comic book", golden oldies constantly playing imanating from a bubbly Wurlitzer, saucy waitresses in bobby socks, menu's with items like the Fats Domino cheeseburger, or the Wolfman Jack omelette, and over prices that pay for all this bullshit.

But then there's "Jackrabbit Slim's", the big mamou of the fifties diners. Either the best or the worst, depending on your point of view.

Vincent's Malibu pulls up to the restaurant. A big sign with a neon figure of a cartoon surly cool cat jackrabbit in a red windbreaker, towers above the establishment. Underneath the cartoon is the name; "Jackrabbit Slim's". Underneath that is the slogan; "Next best thing to a time machine".

*Vincent, getting out of the car looks at the diner *
*in somewhat of a shock. *

* VINCENT *
* What the fuck is this place? *

* MIA *
* It's Jackrabbit Slim's. You look *
* like a fifties boy. A Elvis man *
* should love it. *

* VINCENT *
* C'mon Mia, let's get a steak. *

* MIA *
* You can get a steak here. Hey *
* daddy-o, don't be a... *

*Mia makes the international symbol for square, made *
*popular by Pebbles Flintstone.

* VINCENT *
* After you kitty-kat. *

19. INT. JACKRABBIT SLIM'S – NIGHT 19.

Compared to the interior, the exterior was that of a quaint English pub. Posters from the 50's A.I.P. movies are all over the wall ("ROCK ALL NIGHT", "HIGH SCHOOL CONFIDENTIAL", "ATTACK OF THE CRAB MONSTER", and "MACHINE GUN KELLY"). The booths that the patrons sit in are made out of cut up bodies of 50's cars.

In the middle of the restaurant is a dance floor. A big sign on the wall states, "No shoes allowed". So wannabe beboppers (actually Melrose-types), do the twist in their socks or barefeet.

The picture windows don't look out the street, but instead, B & W movies of 50's street scenes play behind them. The WAITRESSES and WAITERS are made up as replicas of 50's icons: MARILYN MONROE, ZORRO, JAMES DEAN, DONNA REED, MARTIN AND LEWIS, and THE PHILIP MORRIS MIDGET, wait on tables wearing appropriate costumes.

Vincent and Mia study the menu in a booth made out of a red '59 Edsel. BUDDY HOLLY (their waiter), comes over, sporting a big red button on his chest that says: "Hi I'm Buddy, pleasing you pleases me."

BUDDY
Hi I'm Buddy, what can I get'cha?

VINCENT
I'll have the Douglas Sirk steak.

BUDDY
How d'ya want it, burnt to a crisp,
or bloody as hell?

VINCENT
Bloody as hell. And to drink, a vanilla coke.

BUDDY
How 'bout you, Peggy Sue?

MIA
I'll have the Durwood Kirby burger -- bloody -- and a five-dollar shake.

BUDDY
How d'ya want that shake, Martin and Lewis, or Amos and Andy?

MIA
Martin and Lewis.

VINCENT
Did you just order a five-dollar shake?

MIA
Sure did.

VINCENT
A shake? Milk and ice cream?

MIA
Uh-huh.

VINCENT
It cost five dollars?

BUDDY
Yep.

VINCENT
You don't put bourbon in it or anything?

BUDDY
Nope.

VINCENT
Just checking.

Buddy exits.

Vincent takes a look around the place. The YUPPIES are dancing, the DINERS are biting into big, juicy hamburgers, and the icons are playing their parts. Marilyn is squealing, The Midget is paging Philip Morris, Donna Reed is making her customers drink their milk, and Dean and Jerry are acting a fool.

MIA
Whaddya think?

VINCENT
It's like a wax museum with a pulse rate.

Vincent takes out his pouch of tobacco and begins rolling himself a smoke.

After a second of watching him --

MIA
What are you doing?

VINCENT
Rollin' a smoke.

MIA
Here?

VINCENT
It's just tobacco.

MIA
Oh. Well in that case, will you roll me one, cowboy?

As he finishes licking it --

VINCENT
You can have this one, cowgirl.

He hands her the rolled smoke. She takes it, putting it to her lips. Out of nowhere appears a Zippo lighter in Vincent's hand. He lights it.

MIA
Thanks.

VINCENT
Think nothing of it.

He begins rolling one for himself.

At this time, the SOUND of a subway car fills the diner, making everything SHAKE and RATTLE. Marilyn Monroe runs to a square vent in the floor. An imaginary subway train BLOWS the skirt of her white dress around her ears as she lets out a squeal. The entire restaurant applauds.

Back to Mia and Vincent

MIA

So Marsellus tells me you just came back from Amsterdam.

VINCENT

Sure did.

MIA

How long were you there?

VINCENT

A little more than three years.

MIA

I love Amsterdam.

VINCENT

You've been there?

MIA

I go there about once a year and chill out for a month.

VINCENT

No kidding. I didn't know that.

MIA

Why would you? Did you ever go to a hash bar three blocks from the Anne Frank house, the Cobra?

VINCENT

You've been in the Cobra? That's a real small little place. How do you know about the Cobra?

MIA

I've known about the Cobra since Derrick opened it.

VINCENT

You know Derrick?

MIA

I've known Derrick goin' on six years now.

VINCENT
I can't believe this. Me and Derrick
are buddies.

MIA
So are Derrick and I.

VINCENT
This is blowin' my mind. I practically
lived at the Cobra.

MIA
When I'm in Amsterdam, I literally
live at the Cobra. I stay in the house
with Derrick and Petra.

VINCENT
You stay at the Cobra?

MIA
My picture's on the wall.

VINCENT
Where's your picture?

MIA
You know all the pictures Derrick
has up behind the bar?

VINCENT
Yeah.

MIA
There's one of Derrick between two
girls wearing baseball jerseys. Petra's
the one in the baseball cap, and the
one in the cowboy hat is me.

VINCENT
That's you in the cowboy hat?

Mia smiles and nods.

VINCENT (cont'd)
So you're the girl in the cowboy hat.
It's things like this make you realize
how small a planet this is. I couda
took you out. Why didn't Marsellus
hook us up?

* MIA *
* When I go to Amsterdam, I go alone, to *
* be alone. I don't want to be entertained. *
*
* VINCENT *
* I can understand that. I heard you did *
* a pilot. *

MIA
That was my fifteen minutes.

VINCENT
What was it?

MIA
It was a show about a team of female secret agents called "Fox Force Five."

VINCENT
What?

MIA
"Fox Force Five." Fox, as in we're a bunch of foxy chicks. Force, as in we're a force to be reckoned with. Five, as in there's one..two..three..four..five of us. There was a blonde one, Sommerset O'Neal from the show "Baton Rouge," she was the leader. A Japanese one, a black one, a French one and a brunette one, me. We all had special skills. Somerset had a photographic memory, the Japanese fox was a kung fu master, the black girl was a demolition expert, the French fox' specialty was sex....

VINCENT
What was your specialty?

MIA
Knives. The character I played, Raven McCoy, her background was she was raised by circus performers. So she grew up doing a knife act. According to the show, she was the deadliest woman in the world with a knife.
(MORE)

MIA (CONT'D)

But because she grew up in a circus, she was also something of an acrobat. She could do illusions, she was a trapeze artist -- when you're keeping the world safe from evil, you never know when being a trapeze artist's gonna come in handy. And she knew a zillion old jokes her grandfather, an old vaudevillian, taught her. If we woulda got picked up, they woulda worked in a gimmick where every episode I woulda told an old joke.

VINCENT

Do you remember any of the jokes?

MIA

Well I only got the chance to say one, 'cause we only did one show.

VINCENT

Tell me.

MIA

No. It's really corny.

VINCENT

C'mon, don't be that way.

MIA

No. You won't like it and I'll be embarrassed.

VINCENT

You told it in front of fifty million people and you can't tell it to me? I promise I won't laugh.

MIA

(laughing)

That's what I'm afraid of.

VINCENT

That's not what I meant and you know it.

MIA

You're quite the silver tongue devil, aren't you?

VINCENT

I meant I wouldn't laugh at you.

MIA
That's not what you said Vince. Well now I'm definitely not gonna tell ya, 'cause it's been built up too much.

VINCENT
What a gyp.

Buddy comes back with the drinks. Mia wraps her lips around the straw of her shake.

MIA
Yummy!

VINCENT
Can I have a sip of that? I'd like to know what a five-dollar shake tastes like.

MIA
Be my guest.

She slides the shake over to him.

MIA
You can use my straw, I don't have kooties.

Vincent smiles.

VINCENT
Yeah, but maybe I do.

MIA
Kooties I can handle.

He takes a sip.

VINCENT
Goddamn! That's a pretty fuckin' good milk shake.

MIA
Told ya.

VINCENT
I don't know if it's worth five dollars, but it's pretty fuckin' good.

He slides the shake back.

Then the first of an uncomfortable silence happens.

MIA
Don't you hate that?

VINCENT
What?

MIA
Uncomfortable silences. Why do we feel it's necessary to yak about bullshit in order to be comfortable?

VINCENT
I don't know.

MIA
That's when you know you found somebody special. When you can just shut the fuck up for a minute, and comfortably share silence.

VINCENT
I don't think we're there yet. But don't feel bad, we just met each other.

MIA
Well I'll tell you what, I'll go to the bathroom and powder my nose, while you sit here and think of something to say.

VINCENT
I'll do that.

20. INT. JACKRABBIT SLIM'S (LADIES ROOM) – NIGHT 20.

Mia powders her nose by doing a big line of coke off the bathroom sink. Her head jerks up from the rush.

MIA
(imitating Steppenwolf)
I said goddamn!

21. INT. JACKRABBIT SLIM'S (DINING AREA) – NIGHT 21.

Vincent digs into his Douglas Sirk steak. As he chews, his eyes scan the Hellsapopinish restaurant.

Mia comes back to the table.

MIA
Don't you love it when you go to the bathroom and you come back to find your food waiting for you?

VINCENT
We're lucky we got it at all. Buddy Holly doesn't seem to be much of a waiter. We shoulda sat in Marilyn Monroe's section.

MIA
Which one, there's two Marilyn Monroes.

VINCENT
No there's not.

Pointing at Marilyn in the white dress serving a table.

VINCENT
That's Marilyn Monroe...

Then, pointing at a BLONDE WAITRESS in a tight sweater and capri pants, taking an order from a bunch of FILM GEEKS --

VINCENT
...and that's Mamie Van Doren. I don't see Jayne Mansfield, so it must be her night off.

MIA
Pretty smart.

VINCENT
I have moments.

MIA
Did ya think of something to say?

VINCENT
Actually, there's something I've wanted to ask you about, but you seem like a nice person, and I didn't want to offend you.

MIA
Oooohhhh, this doesn't sound like mindless, boring, getting-to-know-you chit-chat. This sounds like you actually have something to say.

VINCENT
Only if you promise not to get offended.

MIA
You can't promise something like that. I have no idea what you're gonna ask. You could ask me what you're gonna ask me, and my natural response could be to be offended. Then, through no fault of my own, I woulda broken my promise.

VINCENT
Then let's just forget it.

MIA
That is an impossibility. Trying to forget anything as intriguing as this would be an exercise in futility.

VINCENT
Is that a fact?

Mia nods her head: "Yes."

MIA
Besides, it's more exciting when you don't have permission.

VINCENT
What do you think about what happened to Antwan?

MIA
Who's Antwan?

VINCENT
Tony Rocky Horror.

MIA
He fell out of a window.

VINCENT
That's one way to say it. Another way is, he was thrown out. Another way is, he was thrown out by Marsellus. And even another way is, he was thrown out of a window by Marsellus because of you.

MIA
Is that a fact?

VINCENT
No it's not, it's just what I heard.

MIA
Who told you this?

VINCENT
They.

Mia and Vincent smile.

MIA
They talk a lot, don't they?

VINCENT
They certainly do.

MIA
Well don't be shy Vincent, what exactly did they say?

Vincent is slow to answer.

MIA
Let me help you Bashful, did it involve the F-word?

VINCENT
No. They just said Rocky Horror gave you a foot massage.

MIA
And...?

VINCENT
No and, that's it.

MIA
You heard Marsellus threw Rocky Horror out of a four-story window because he massaged my feet?

VINCENT
Yeah.

MIA
And you believed that?

VINCENT
At the time I was told, it seemed reasonable.

MIA

Marsellus throwing Tony out of a four-story window for giving me a foot massage seemed reasonable?

VINCENT

No, it seemed excessive. But that doesn't mean it didn't happen. I heard Marsellus is very protective of you.

MIA

A husband being protective of his wife is one thing. A husband almost killing another man for touching his wife's feet is something else.

VINCENT

But did it happen?

MIA

The only thing Antwan ever touched of mine was my hand, when he shook it. I met Anwan once -- at my wedding -- then never again. The truth is, nobody knows why Marsellus tossed Tony Rocky Horror out of that window except Marsellus and Tony Rocky Horror. But when you scamps get together, you're worse than a sewing circle.

VINCENT

Are you mad?

MIA

Not at all. Being the subject of back-fence gossip goes with the ring, I guess.

She takes a sip of her five-dollar shake, and says:

MIA

Thanks.

VINCENT

What for?

MIA

Asking my side.

At that moment, a great oldie-but-goodie BLASTS from the jukebox.

MIA
I wanna dance.

VINCENT
I'm not much of a dancer.

MIA
Now I'm the one gettin' gyped. I do believe Marsellus told you to take me out and do whatever I wanted. Well, now I want to dance.

Vincent smiles and begins taking off his boots. Mia triumphantly casts hers off. He takes her hand, escorting her to the dance floor. The two face each other for that brief moment before you begin to dance, then they both break into a devilish twist. Mia's version of the twist is that of a sexy cat. Vincent is pure Mr. Cool as he gets into a hip-swivelling rhythm that would make Mr. Checker proud.

The OTHER DANCERS on the floor are trying to do the same thing, but Vincent and Mia seem to be strangely shaking their asses in sync. The two definitely share a rhythm and share smiles as they SING ALONG with the last verse of the Golden Oldie.

CUT TO:

22. INT. MARSELLUS WALLACE'S HOME – NIGHT 22.

The front door FLINGS open, and Mia and Vincent dance tango-style into the house, singing a cappella the song from the previous scene. They finish their little dance, laughing.

Then....

The two just stand face to face looking at each other.

VINCENT
Was that an uncomfortable silence?

MIA
I don't know what that was.
(pause)
Music and drinks!

Mia moves away to attend to both. Vincent hangs up his overcoat on a big bronze coat rack in the alcove.

VINCENT
I'm gonna take a piss.

MIA
That was a little bit more information than I needed to know, but go right ahead.

Vincent shuffles off to the john.

Mia moves to her CD player, thumbs through a stack of CDs and selects one: k.d. lang. The speakers BLAST OUT a high energy country number, which Mia plays air-guitar to. She dances her way around the room and finds herself by Vincent's overcoat hanging on the rack. She touches its sleeve. It feels good.

Her hand goes in its pocket and pulls out his tobacco pouch. Like a little girl playing cowboy, she spreads the tobacco on some rolling paper. Imitating what he did earlier, licks the paper and rolls it into a pretty good cigarette. Maybe a little too fat, but not bad for a first try. Mia thinks so anyway. Her hand reaches back in the pocket and pulls out his Zippo lighter. She SLAPS the lighter against her leg, trying to light it fancy-style like Vince did. What do you know, she did it! Mia's one happy clam. She triumphantly brings the fat flame up to her fat smoke, lighting it up, then LOUDLY SNAPS the Zippo closed.

The Mia-made cigarette is brought up to her lips, and she takes a long, cool drag. Her hand slides the Zippo back in the overcoat pocket. But wait, her fingers touch something else. Those fingers bring out a plastic bag with white powder inside, the madman that Vincent bought earlier from Lance. Wearing a big smile, Mia brings the bag of heroin up to her face.

MIA
(like you would say Bingo!)
Disco! Vince, you little cola nut, you've been holding out on me.

CUT TO:

23. INT. BATHROOM (MARSELLUS WALLACE'S HOUSE) – NIGHT 23.

Vincent stands at the sink, washing his hands, talking to himself in the mirror.

VINCENT
One drink and leave. Don't be rude, but drink your drink quickly, say goodbye, walk out the door, get in your car, and go down the road.

LIVING ROOM
Mia has the unbeknownst-to-her heroin cut up into big lines on her glass top coffee table. Taking her trusty hundred dollar bill like a human Dust-Buster, she quickly snorts the fat line.

CU – MIA
her head JERKS back. Her hands go to her nose (which feels like it's on fucking fire), something is terribly wrong. Then...the rush hits....

BATHROOM
Vincent dries his hands on a towel while he continues his dialogue with the mirror.

VINCENT
...it's a moral test of yourself, whether or not you can maintain loyalty. Because when people are loyal to each other, that's very meaningful.

LIVING ROOM
Mia is on all fours trying to crawl to the bathroom, but it's like she's trying to crawl with the bones removed from her knees. Blood begins to drip from Mia's nose. Then her stomach gets into the act and she VOMITS.

BATHROOM
Vince continues.

VINCENT
So you're gonna go out there, drink your drink, say "Goodnight, I've had a very lovely evening," go home, and jack off. And that's all you're gonna do.

Now that he's given himself a little pep talk, Vincent's ready for whatever's waiting for him on the other side of that door. So he goes through it.

LIVING ROOM
We follow behind Vincent as he walks from the bathroom to the living room, where he finds Mia lying on the floor like a rag doll. She's twisted on her back. Blood and puke are down her front. And her face is contorted. Not out of the tightness of pain, but just the opposite, the muscles in her face are so

relaxed, she lies still with her mouth wide open. Slack-jawed.

VINCENT
Jesus Christ!

Vincent moves like greased lightning to Mia's fallen body. Bending down where she lays, he puts his fingers on her neck to check her pulse. She slightly stirs.

Mia is aware of Vincent over her, speaking to her.

VINCENT
(sounding weird)
Mia! Mia! What the hell happened?

But she's unable to communicate. Mia makes a few lost mumbles, but they're not distinctive enough to be called words.

Vincent props her eyelids open and sees the story.

VINCENT
(to himself)
I'll be a sonofabitch.
(to Mia)
Mia! Mia! What did you take?
Answer me honey, what did you take?

Mia is incapable of answering. He SLAPS her face hard.

Vincent SPRINGS up and RUNS to his overcoat, hanging on the rack. He goes through the pockets FRANTICALLY. It's gone. Vincent makes a beeline to Mia. We follow.

VINCENT
(yelling to Mia)
Okay honey, we're getting you on your feet.

He reaches her and hoists the dead weight up in his arms.

VINCENT
We're on our feet now, and now we're gonna walk out to the car. Here we go, watch us walk.

We follow behind as he hurriedly walks the practically-unconscious Mia through the house and out the front door.

24. EXT. VINCENT'S HOT ROD (MOVING) — NIGHT 24.

INSERT SPEEDOMETER: red needle on a hundred.

Vincent driving like a madman in a town without traffic laws, speeds the car into turns and up and over hills.

25. INT. VINCENT'S HOT ROD (MOVING) – NIGHT 25.

Vincent, one hand firmly on the wheel, the other shifting like Robocop, both eyes staring straight ahead except when he glances over at Mia.

Mia, slack-jawed expression, mouth gaping, posture of a bag of water.

Vincent takes a cellular phone out of his pocket. He punches a number.

26. INT. LANCE'S HOUSE – NIGHT 26.

At this late hour, Lance has transformed from a bon vivant drug dealer to a bathrobe creature.

He sits in a big comfy chair, ratty blue gym pants, a worn-out but comfortable tee-shirt that has, written on it, "TAFT, CALIFORNIA," and a moth-ridden terry cloth robe. In his hand is a bowl of Cap'n Crunch with Crunch Berries. In front of him on the coffee table is a jug of milk, the box the Cap'n Crunch with Crunch Berries came out of, and a hash pipe in an ashtray.

On the big-screen TV in front of the table is the Three Stooges, and they're getting married.

PREACHER (EMIL SIMKUS)
(on TV)
Hold hands, you love birds.

The phone RINGS.

Lance puts down his cereal and makes his way to the phone.

It RINGS again.

Jody, his wife, CALLS from the bedroom, obviously woken up.

JODY (OS)
Lance! The phone's ringing!

LANCE
(calling back)
I can hear it!

JODY (OS)
I thought you told those fuckin' assholes never to call this late!

LANCE
(by the phone)
I told 'em and that's what I'm gonna tell this fuckin' asshole right now!
(he answers the phone)
Hello, do you know how late it is? You're not supposed to be callin' me this fuckin' late.

BACK TO VINCENT IN THE MALIBU
Vincent is still driving like a stripe-assed ape, clutching the phone to his ear. WE CUT BACK AND FORTH during the conversation.

VINCENT
Lance, this is Vincent, I'm in big fuckin' trouble man, I'm on my way to your place.

LANCE
Whoa, hold your horses man, what's the problem?

VINCENT
You still got an adrenalin shot?

LANCE
(dawning on him)
Maybe.

VINCENT
I need it man, I got a chick she's fuckin' O.D.ing on me.

LANCE
Don't bring her here! I'm not even fuckin' joking with you, don't you be bringing some fucked up pooh-butt to my house!

VINCENT
No choice.

LANCE
She's O.D.in'?

VINCENT
Yeah. She's dyin'.

LANCE
Then bite the fuckin' bullet, take 'er to a hospital and call a lawyer!

VINCENT
Negative.

LANCE
She ain't my fuckin' problem, you fucked her up, you deal with it -- are you talkin' to me on a cellular phone?

VINCENT
Sorry.

LANCE
I don't know you, who is this, don't come here, I'm hangin' up.

VINCENT
Too late, I'm already here.

At that moment inside Lance's house, WE HEAR Vincent's Malibu coming up the street. Lance hangs up the phone, goes to his curtains and YANKS the cord. The curtains open with a WHOOSH in time to see Vincent's Malibu DRIVING UP on his front lawn and CRASHING into his house. The window Lance is looking out of SHATTERS from the impact.

JODY (OS)
What the hell was that?

Lance CHARGES from the window, out the door to his front lawn.

27. EXT. LANCE'S HOUSE – NIGHT 27.

Vincent is already out of the car, working on getting Mia out.

LANCE
Have you lost your mind?! You crashed your car in my fuckin' house! You talk about drug shit on a cellular fuckin' phone --

VINCENT
If you're through havin' your little hissy fit, this chick is dyin', get your needle and git it now!

LANCE
Are you deaf? You're not bringin' that fucked up bitch in my house!

VINCENT
This fucked up bitch is Marsellus Wallace's wife. Now if she fuckin' croaks on me, I'm a grease spot. But before he turns me into a bar soap, I'm gonna be forced to tell 'im about how you coulda saved her life, but instead you let her die on your front lawn.

28. INT. LANCE'S HOUSE – NIGHT 28.

WE START in Lance's and Jody's bedroom.

Jody, in bed, throws off the covers and stands up. She's wearing a long tee-shirt with a picture of Fred Flintstone on it.

We follow HANDHELD behind her as she opens the door, walking through the hall into the living room.

JODY
It's only one-thirty in the goddamn mornin'! What the fuck's goin' on out here?!

As she walks in the living room, she sees Vincent and Lance standing over Mia, who's lying on the floor in the middle of the room.

From here on in, everything in this scene is frantic, like a DOCUMENTARY in an emergency ward, with the big difference here being nobody knows what the fuck they're doing.

JODY
Who's she?

Lance looks up at Jody.

LANCE
Get that black box in the bedroom I have with the adrenalin shot.

JODY
What's wrong with her?

VINCENT
She's O.D.ing on us.

JODY
Well get her the hell outta here!

LANCE AND VINCENT
(in stereo)
Get the fuckin' shot!

JODY
Don't yell at me!

She angrily turns and disappears into the bedroom looking for the shot.

WE MOVE into the room with the two men.

VINCENT
(to Lance)
You two are a match made in heaven.

LANCE
Look, just keep talkin' to her, okay? While she's gettin' the shot, I gotta get a medical book.

VINCENT
What do you need a medical book for?

LANCE
To tell me how to do it. I've never given an adrenalin shot before.

VINCENT
You've had that thing for six years and you never used it?

LANCE
I never had to use it. I don't go joy-poppin' with bubble-gummers, all of my friends can handle their highs!

VINCENT
Well then get it.

LANCE
I am, if you'll let me.

VINCENT
I'm not fuckin' stoppin' you.

LANCE
Stop talkin' to me, and start talkin' to her.

WE FOLLOW Lance as he runs out of the living room into a...

29. SPARE ROOM 29.

with a bunch of junk in it. He frantically starts scanning the junk for the book he's looking for, repeating the words, "Come on," endlessly.

From OFF SCREEN we hear:

VINCENT (OS)
Hurry up man! We're losin' her!

LANCE
(calling back)
I'm looking as fast as I can!

Lance continues his frenzied search.

WE HEAR Jody in the living room now as she talks to Vincent.

JODY (OS)
What's he lookin' for?

VINCENT (OS)
I dunno, some medical book.

Jody calls to Lance.

JODY (OS)
What are you lookin' for?

LANCE
My black medical book!

As he continues searching, flipping and knocking over shit, Jody appears in the doorway.

JODY
What are you looking for?

LANCE
My black fuckin' medical book. It's like a text book they give to nurses.

JODY
I never saw a medical book.

LANCE
Trust me, I have one.

JODY
Well if it's that important, why didn't you keep it with the shot?

Lance spins toward her.

LANCE
I don't know! Stop bothering me!

JODY
While you're lookin' for it, that girl's gonna die on our carpet. You're never gonna find it in all this shit. For six months now, I've been tellin' you to clean this room --

VINCENT (OS)
-- get your ass in here, fuck the book!

Lance angrily knocks over a pile of shit and leaves the SHOT heading for the living room.

30. LIVING ROOM 30.

Vincent is bent over Mia, talking softly to her, when Lance reenters the room.

VINCENT
Quit fuckin' around man and give her the shot!

Lance bends down by the black case brought in by Jody. He opens it and begins preparing the needle for injection.

LANCE
While I'm doing this, take her shirt off and find her heart.

Vincent rips her blouse open.

Jody stumbles back in the room, hanging back from the action.

VINCENT
Does it have to be exact?

LANCE
Yeah, it has to be exact! I'm giving her an injection in the heart, so I gotta exactly hit her in the heart.

VINCENT
Well, I don't know exactly where her heart is, I think it's here.

Vince points to Mia's right breast. Lance glances over and nods.

LANCE
That's it.

As Lance readies the injection, Vincent looks up at Jody.

VINCENT
I need a big fat magic marker, got one?

JODY
What?

VINCENT
I need a big fat magic marker, any felt pen'll do, but a magic marker would be great.

JODY
Hold on.

Jody runs to the desk, opens the top drawer and, in her enthusiasm, she pulls the drawer out of the desk, the content of which (bills, papers, pens) spill to the floor.

The injection is ready. Lance hands Vincent the needle.

LANCE
It's ready, I'll tell you what to do.

VINCENT
You're gonna give her the shot.

LANCE
No, you're gonna give her the shot.

VINCENT
I've never done this before.

LANCE
I've never done this before either, and I ain't startin' now. You brought 'er here, that means you give her the shot. The day I bring an O.D.ing bitch to your place, then I gotta give her the shot.

Jody hurriedly joins them in the huddle, a big fat red magic marker in her hand.

JODY
Got it.

Vincent grabs the magic marker out of Jody's hand and makes a big red dot on Mia's body where her heart is.

VINCENT
Okay, what do I do?

LANCE
Well, you're giving her an injection of adrenalin straight to her heart. But she's got a breast plate in front of her heart, so you gotta pierce through that. So what you gotta do is bring the needle down in a stabbing motion.

Lance demonstrates a stabbing motion, which looks like "The Shape" killing its victims in "HALLOWEEN."

VINCENT
I gotta stab her?

LANCE
If you want the needle to pierce through to her heart, you gotta stab her hard. Then once you do, push down on the plunger.

VINCENT
What happens after that?

LANCE
I'm curious about that myself.

VINCENT
This ain't a fuckin' joke man!

LANCE
She's supposed to come out of it like --
(snaps his fingers)
-- that.

Vincent lifts the needle up above his head in a stabbing motion. He looks down on Mia.

Mia is fading fast. Soon nothing will help her.

Vincent's eyes narrow, ready to do this.

VINCENT
Count to three.

Lance, on his knees right beside Vincent, does not know what to expect.

LANCE
One...

RED DOT on Mia's body.

Needle raised ready to strike.

LANCE (OS)
...two...

Jody's face is alive with anticipation.

NEEDLE in the air, poised like a rattler ready to strike.

LANCE (OS)
...three!

The needle leaves frame, THRUSTING down hard.

Vincent brings the needle down hard, STABBING Mia in the chest.

Mia's head is JOLTED from the impact.

The syringe plunger is pushed down, PUMPING the adrenalin out through the needle.

Mia's eyes POP WIDE OPEN and she lets out a HELLISH cry of the banshee. She BOLTS UP in a sitting position, needle stuck in her chest -- SCREAMING.

Vincent, Lance and Jody, who were in sitting positions in front of Mia, JUMP BACK, scared to death.

Mia's scream runs out. She slowly starts taking breaths of air.

The other three, now scooted halfway across the room, shaken to their bones, look to see if she's alright.

LANCE
If you're okay, say something.

Mia, still breathing, not looking up at them, says in a relatively normal voice.

MIA
Something.

Vincent and Lance collapse on their backs, exhausted and shaking from how close to death Mia came.

JODY
Anybody want a beer?

CUT TO:

31. INT. VINCENT'S MALIBU (MOVING) – NIGHT 31.

Vincent is behind the wheel driving Mia home. No one says anything, both are still too shaken.

32. EXT. FRONT OF MARSELLUS WALLACE'S HOUSE – NIGHT 32.

The Malibu pulls up to the front. Mia gets out without saying a word (still in a daze) and begins walking down the walkway toward her front door.

VINCENT (OS)
Mia!

She turns around.

Vincent's out of the car, standing on the walkway, a big distance between the two.

VINCENT
What are your thoughts on how to handle this?

MIA
What's yours?

VINCENT
Well I'm of the opinion that Marsellus can live his whole life and never ever hear of this incident.

Mia smiles.

MIA
Don't worry about it. If Marsellus ever heard of this, I'd be in as much trouble as you.

VINCENT
I seriously doubt that.

MIA
If you can keep a secret, so can I.

VINCENT
Let's shake on it.

The two walk toward each other, holding out their hands to shake and shake they do.

VINCENT
Mum's the word.

Mia lets go of Vincent's hand and silently makes the see-no-evil, hear-no-evil, and speak-no-evil sign with her hands.

Vincent smiles.

VINCENT
If you'll excuse me, I gotta go home and have a heart attack.

Mia giggles.

Vincent turns to leave.

MIA
You still wanna hear my "FOX FORCE FIVE" joke?

Vincent turns around.

VINCENT
Sure, but I think I'm still a little too petrified to laugh.

MIA
Uh-huh. You won't laugh because it's not funny. But if you still wanna hear it, I'll tell it.

VINCENT
I can't wait.

MIA
Three tomatoes are walking down the street, a poppa tomato, a momma tomato, and a little baby tomato. The baby tomato is lagging behind the poppa and momma tomato. The poppa tomato gets mad, goes over to the momma tomato and stamps on him --
(STAMPS the ground)
-- and says: catch up.

They both smile, but neither laugh.

MIA
See ya 'round, Vince.

Mia turns and walks inside her house.

CU – VINCENT
after Mia walks inside. Vincent continues to look at where she was. He brings his hands to his lips and blows her a kiss. Then exits FRAME leaving it empty. WE HEAR his Malibu START UP and DRIVE AWAY.

FADE TO BLACK

33. FADE UP: 33.

ON THE CARTOON "SPEED RACER."
Speed is giving a detailed description of all the features on his race car "The Mac-5," which he does at the beginning of every episode.

OFF SCREEN we hear a WOMAN'S VOICE....

WOMAN'S VOICE (OS)
Butch.

DISSOLVE TO:

BUTCH'S POV
We're in the living room of a modest two bedroom house in Alhambra, California, in the year 1972.
BUTCH'S MOTHER, 35ish, stands in the doorway leading into the living room. Next to her is a man dressed in the uniform of an American Air Force officer. The CAMERA is the perspective of a five-year old boy.

MOTHER
Butch, stop watching TV a second. We got a special visitor. Now do you remember when I told you your daddy died in a P.O.W. camp?

BUTCH (OS)
Uh-huh.

MOTHER
Well this here is Capt. Koons. He was in the P.O.W. camp with Daddy.

CAPT. KOONS steps inside the room toward the little boy and bends down on one knee to bring him even with the boy's eyeline. When Koons speaks, he speaks with a slight Texas accent.

CAPT. KOON

Hello, little man. Boy I sure heard a bunch about you. See, I was a good friend of your Daddy's. We were in that Hanoi pit of hell over five years together. Hopefully, you'll never have to experience this yourself, but when two men are in a situation like me and your Daddy were, for as long as we were, you take on certain responsibilities of the other. If it had been me who had not made it, Major Coolidge would be talkin' right now to my son Jim. But the way it worked out is I'm talkin' to you, Butch. I got somethin' for ya.

The Captain pulls a gold wrist watch out of his pocket.

CAPT. KOONS

This watch I got here was first purchased by your great-granddaddy. It was bought during the First World War in a little general store in Knoxville, Tennessee. It was bought by private Doughboy Erine Coolidge the day he set sail for Paris. It was your great-granddaddy's war watch, made by the first company to ever make wrist watches. You see, up until then, people just carried pocket watches. Your great-granddaddy wore that watch every day he was in the war. Then when he had done his duty, he went home to your great-grandmother, took the watch off his wrist and put it in an ol' coffee can. And in that can it stayed 'til your grandfather Dane Coolidge was called upon by his country to go overseas and fight the Germans once again. This time they called it World War Two.

(MORE)

CAPT. KOON (CONT'D)

Your great-granddaddy gave it to your granddad for good luck. Unfortunately, Dane's luck wasn't as good as his old man's. Your granddad was a Marine and he was killed with all the other Marines at the battle of Wake Island. Your granddad was facing death and he knew it. None of those boys had any illusions about ever leavin' that island alive. So three days before the Japanese took the island, your 22-year old grandfather asked a gunner on an Air Force transport named Winocki, a man he had never met before in his life, to deliver to his infant son, who he had never seen in the flesh, his gold watch. Three days later, your grandfather was dead. But Winocki kept his word. After the war was over, he paid a visit to your grandmother, delivering to your infant father, his Dad's gold watch. This watch. This watch was on your Daddy's wrist when he was shot down over Hanoi. He was captured and put in a Vietnamese prison camp. Now he knew if the gooks ever saw the watch it'd be confiscated. The way your Daddy looked at it, that watch was your birthright. And he'd be damned if any slopeheads were gonna put their greasy yella hands on his boy's birthright. So he hid it in the one place he knew he could hide somethin'. His ass. Five long years, he wore this watch up his ass. Then when he died of dysentery, he gave me the watch. I hid this uncomfortable hunk of metal up my ass for two years. Then, after seven years, I was sent home to my family. And now, little man, I give the watch to you.

Capt. Koons hands the watch to Butch. A little hand comes into FRAME to accept it.

CUT TO:

34. INT. LOCKER ROOM – NIGHT 34.

The 27-year old Butch Coolidge is dressed in boxing regalia: trunks, shoes and gloves. He lies on a table catching a few zzzzzz's before his big fight. Almost as soon as WE CUT to him, he wakes up with a start. Shaken by the bizarre memory, he wipes his sweaty face with his boxing glove.

His trainer KLONDIKE, an older fireplug, opens the door a little, sticking his head in the room. Pandemonium seems to be breaking out behind Klondike in the hallway.

KLONDIKE
It's time, Butch.

BUTCH
I'm ready.

Klondike steps inside, closing the door on the WILD MOB outside. He goes to the long yellow robe hanging on a hook. Butch hops off the table and, without a word, Klondike helps him on with the robe, which says on the back: "BATTLING BUTCH COOLIDGE."

The two men head for the door. Klondike opens the door for Butch. As Butch steps into the hallway, the Crowd goes apeshit. Klondike closes the door behind him, leaving us in the quiet, empty locker room.

FADE TO BLACK

TITLE CARD:

"THE GOLD WATCH"

WE HEAR OVER THE BLACK AND TITLE:

SPORTSCASTER #1 (OS)
-- well Dan, that had to be the bloodiest and, hands-down, the most brutal fight this city has ever seen.

The SOUND of chaos in the b.g.

FADE IN:

35. EXT. ALLEY (RAINING) – NIGHT 35.

A taxi is parked in a dark alley next to an auditorium. The sky is PISSIN' DOWN RAIN. WE SLOWLY DOLLY toward the parked car. The SOUND of the CAR RADIO can be heard coming from inside.

SPORTSCASTER #1 (OS)
...Coolidge was out of there faster than I've ever seen a victorious boxer vacate the ring. Do you think he knew Willis was dead?

SPORTSCASTER #2 (OS)
My guess would be yes, Richard. I could see from my position here, the frenzy in his eyes give way to the realization of what he was doing. I think any man would've left the ring that fast.

DISSOLVE TO:

36. INT. TAXI (PARKED/RAINING) – NIGHT 36.

Inside the taxi, behind the wheel, is a female cabbie named ESMARELDA VILLALOBOS. A young woman, with Spanish looks, sits parked, drinking a steaming hot cup of coffee out of a white styrofoam cup.

The Sportscasters continue their coverage.

SPORTSCASTER #1 (OS)
Do you feel this ring death tragedy will have an effect on the world of boxing?

SPORTSCASTER #2 (OS)
Oh Dan, a tragedy like this can't help but shake the world of boxing to its very foundation. But it's of paramount importance that during the sad weeks ahead, the eyes of the W.B.A. remain firmly fixed on the -- CLICK --

Esmarelda shuts off the radio.

She takes a sip of coffee, then hears a NOISE behind her in the alley. She sticks her head out of the car door to see:

37. A window about three stories high opens on the auditorium-side of the alley. A gym bag is tossed out into a garbage dumpster below the window. Then, Butch Coolidge, still dressed in boxing trunks, shoes, gloves and yellow robe, LEAPS to the dumpster below.

ESMARELDA'S REACTION takes in the strangeness of this sight.

Gym bag in hand, Butch CLIMBS out of the dumpster and RUNS to the taxi. Before he climbs in, he takes off his robe and throws it to the ground.

38. INT. TAXI (PARKED/RAINING) – NIGHT 38.

Butch, soaking wet, naked except for trunks, shoes and gloves, HOPS in the backseat, SLAMMING the door.

Esmarelda, staring straight ahead, talks to Butch through the rearview mirror:

ESMARELDA
(Spanish accent)
Are you the man I was supposed to pick up?

BUTCH
If you're the cab I called, I'm the guy you're supposed to pick up.

ESMARELDA
Where to?

BUTCH
Outta here.

The ignition key is TWISTED. The engine ROARS to life.

The meter is FLIPPED on.

Esmarelda's bare foot STOMPS on the gas pedal.

39. EXT. BOXING AUDITORIUM (RAINING) – NIGHT 39.

The cab WHIPS out of the alley, FISH-TAILING on the wet pavement in front of the auditorium at a rapid pace.

40. INT. WILLIS LOCKER ROOM (AUDITORIUM) – NIGHT 40.

Locker room door opens, English Dave fights his way through the pandemonium which is going on outside in the hall, shutting the door on the madness. Once inside, English Dave takes time to adjust his suit and tie.

In the room, black boxer FLOYD RAY WILLIS lies on a table -- dead. His face looks like he went dunking for bees. His TRAINER is on his knees, head on Floyd's chest, crying over
*the body. He mutters to himself: *

* TRAINER *
* Sweet Jesus, forgive 'em...Sweet *
* Jesus, forgive 'em...never shoulda *
* done it...never shoulda done it... *

The huge figure that is Marsellus Wallace stands at the table, hand on the Trainer's shoulder, lending emotional support. We still do not see Marsellus clearly, only that he is big.

Mia sits in a chair at the far end of the room.

* ENGLISH DAVE *
* Marsellus. *

*ENGLISH DAVES POV: *
*The figure across the room turns towards Dave, with his *
*hand he beckons Mia over. *

* MARSELLUS *
* (To Trainer) *
* English Daves here. I gotta speak *
* with him, but I ain't goin anywhere, *
* I'll be right back. *

*Mia bends down by The Trainer putting her arm *
*around him. *

*MEDIUM ENGLISH DAVE. *
*Marsellus walks up to him. *

MARSELLUS
Whatch got?

ENGLISH DAVE
He booked.

MARSELLUS
* His trainer? *

* ENGLISH DAVE *
* Says he don't know nothin. I believe *
* him. I think Butch surprised his ass *
* same as us. *

MARSELLUS
* We don't wanna think, we wanna know. *
* Take 'em to the kennel, sic the dogs *
* on his ass. We'll find out for *
* goddamn sure what he knows and what *
* he don't.

ENGLISH DAVE
* Butch's search, how ya want it handled? *

MARSELLUS (OS)
I'm prepared to scour the earth for this motherfucker. If Butch goes to Indo China, I want a nigger hidin' in a bowl of rice,
ready to pop a cap in his ass.

ENGLISH DAVE
I'll take care of it.

41. INT. CAB (MOVING/RAINING) – NIGHT 41.

Butch gets one of his boxing gloves off.

Esmarelda watches in the rearview mirror.

He tries to roll down one of the backseat windows, but can't find the roll bar.

BUTCH
Hey, how do I open the window back here?

ESMARELDA
I have to do it.

She presses a button and the back window moves down. Butch tosses his boxing glove out the window, then starts untying the other one.

Esmarelda can't keep quiet anymore.

ESMARELDA
Hey, mister?

BUTCH
(still working on the glove)
What?

ESMARELDA
You were in that fight? The fight on the radio -- you're the fighter?

As he tosses his other glove out the window.

BUTCH
Whatever gave you that idea?

ESMARELDA
No c'mon, you're him, I know you're him, tell me you're him.

BUTCH
(drying himself with a gym towel)
I'm him.

ESMARELDA
You killed the other boxing man.

BUTCH
He's dead?

ESMARELDA
The radio said he was dead.

He finishes wiping himself down.

BUTCH
(to himself)
Sorry 'bout that, Floyd.

He tosses the towel out the window.

Silence, as Butch digs in his bag for a tee-shirt.

ESMARELDA
What does it feel like?

BUTCH
(finds his shirt)
What does what feel like?

ESMARELDA
Killing a man. Beating another man to death with your bare hands.

Butch pulls on his tee-shirt.

BUTCH
Are you some kinda weirdo?

ESMARELDA
No, it's a subject I have much interest in. You are the first person I ever met who has killed somebody. So, what was it like to kill a man?

BUTCH
Tell ya what, you give me one of them cigarettes, I'll give you an answer.

elda bounces in her seat with excitement.

ESMARELDA
Deal!

Butch leans forward. Esmarelda, keeping her eyes on the road, passes a cigarette back to him. He takes it. Then, still not looking behind her, she brings up her hand, a lit match in it. Butch lights his smoke, then blows out the match.

He takes a long drag.

BUTCH
So....

He looks at her license.

BUTCH
...Esmarelda Villalobos -- is that Mexican?

ESMARELDA
The name is Spanish, but I'm Colombian.

BUTCH
It's a very pretty name.

ESMARELDA
It means "Esmarelda of the wolves."

BUTCH
That's one hell of a name you got there, sister.

ESMARELDA
Thank you. And what is your name?

BUTCH
Butch.

ESMARELDA
Butch. What does it mean?

BUTCH
I'm an American, our names don't mean shit. Anyway, moving right along, what is it you wanna know, Esmarelda?

ESMARELDA
I want to know what it feels like to kill a man --

BUTCH
-- I couldn't tell ya. I didn't know he was dead 'til you told me he was dead. Now I know he's dead, do you wanna know how I feel about it?

Esmarelda nods her head: "yes."

BUTCH
I don't feel the least little bit bad. You wanna know why, Esmarelda?

Esmarelda nods her head: "yes."

BUTCH
'Cause I'm a boxer. And after you've said that, you've said pretty much all there is to say about me. Now maybe that son-of-a-bitch tonight was once at one time a boxer. If he was, then he was dead before his ass ever stepped in the ring. I just put the poor bastard outta his misery. And if he never was a boxer --
(Butch takes a drag)
That's what he gets for fuckin' up my sport.

42. EXT. PHONE BOOTH (RAINING) — NIGHT 42.

We DOLLY around a phone booth as Butch talks inside.

BUTCH
(into phone)
What'd I tell ya, soon as the word got out a fix was in, the odds would be outta control.

BUTCH (CONT'D)
Hey, if he was a better fighter he'd be alive. If he never laced up his gloves in the first place, which he never shoulda done, he'd be alive. Enough about the poor unfortunate Mr. Floyd, let's talk about the rich and prosperous Mr. Butch. How many bookies you spread it around with?
(pause)
Eight? How long to collect?
(pause)
So by tomorrow evening, you'll have it all?
(pause)
Good news Scotty, real good news -- I understand a few stragglers aside. Me an' Fabian're gonna leave in the morning. It should take us a couple days to get into Knoxville. Next time we see each other, it'll be on Tennessee time.

Butch hangs up the phone. He looks at the cab waiting to take him wherever he wants to go.

BUTCH
(to himself in French with English subtitles)
Fabian my love, our adventure begins.

CUT TO:

43. EXT. MOTEL (STOPPED RAINING) — NIGHT 43.

Esmarelda's taxi pulls into the motel parking lot. The rain has stopped, but the night is still soaked. Butch gets out, now fully dressed in tee-shirt, jeans and high school athletic jacket. He leans in the driver's side window.

ESMARELDA
Forty-five sixty.

Handing her the money.

BUTCH
Merci beaucoup. And here's a little something for the effort.

Butch holds up a hundred dollar bill.

Esmarelda's eyes light up. She goes to take it. Butch holds it out of reach.

BUTCH
Now if anybody should ask you about who your fare was tonight, what're you gonna tell 'em?

ESMARELDA
The truth. Three well-dressed, slightly toasted, Mexicans.

He gives her the bill.

BUTCH
Bonsoir, Esmarelda.

ESMARELDA
(in Spanish)
Sleep well, Butch.

He tweaks her nose, she smiles, and he turns and walks away. She drives off.

44. INT. MOTEL (ROOM SIX) – NIGHT 44.

Butch enters and turns on the light.

Lying curled up on the bed, fully dressed, with her back to us is Butch's French girlfriend, FABIAN.

FABIAN
Keep the light off.

Butch flicks the switch back, making the room dark again.

BUTCH
Is that better, sugar pop?

FABIAN
Oui. Hard day at the office?

BUTCH
Pretty hard. I got into a fight.

FABIAN
Poor baby. Can we make spoons?

Butch climbs into bed, spooning Fabian from behind.

When Butch and Fabian speak to each other, they speak in baby-talk.

FABIAN
I was looking at myself in the mirror.

BUTCH
Uh-huh?

FABIAN
I wish I had a pot.

BUTCH
You were lookin' in the mirror and you wish you had some pot?

FABIAN
A pot. A pot belly. Pot bellies are sexy.

BUTCH
Well you should be happy, 'cause you do.

FABIAN
Shut up, Fatso! I don't have a pot! I have a bit of a tummy, like Madonna when she did "Lucky Star," it's not the same thing.

BUTCH
I didn't realize there was a difference between a tummy and a pot belly.

FABIAN
The difference is huge.

BUTCH
You want me to have a pot?

FABIAN
No. Pot bellies make a man look either oafish, or like a gorilla. But on a woman, a pot belly is very sexy. The rest of you is normal. Normal face, normal legs, normal hips, normal ass, but with a big, perfectly round pot belly. If I had one, I'd wear a tee-shirt two sizes too small to accentuate it.

BUTCH
You think guys would find that attractive?

FABIAN
I don't give a damn what men find attractive. It's unfortunate what we find pleasing to the touch and pleasing to the eye is seldom the same.

BUTCH
If I had a pot belly, I'd punch you in it.

FABIAN
You'd punch me in my belly?

BUTCH
Right in the belly.

FABIAN
I'd smother you. I'd drop it on your right on your face 'til you couldn't breathe.

BUTCH
You'd do that to me?

FABIAN
Yes!

BUTCH
Did you get everything, sugar pop?

FABIAN
Yes, I did.

BUTCH
Good job.

FABIAN
Did everything go as planned?

BUTCH
You didn't listen to the radio?

FABIAN
I never listen to your fights. Were you the winner?

BUTCH
I won alright.

FABIAN
Are you still retiring?

BUTCH
Sure am.

FABIAN
What about the man you fought?

BUTCH
Floyd retired too.

FABIAN
(smiling)
Really?! He won't be fighting no more?!

BUTCH
Not no more.

FABIAN
So it all worked out in the finish?

BUTCH
We ain't at the finish yet, baby.

Fabian rolls over and Butch gets on top of her. They kiss.

FABIAN
We're in a lot of danger, aren't we?

Butch nods his head: "yes."

FABIAN
If they find us, they'll kill us, won't they?

Butch nods his head: "yes."

FABIAN
But they won't find us, will they?

Butch nods his head: "no."

FABIAN
Do you still want me to go with you?

Butch nods his head: "yes."

FABIAN
I don't want to be a burden or a nuisance --

Butch's hand goes out of frame and starts massaging her crotch.

Fabian reacts.

FABIAN
Say it!

BUTCH
Fabian, I want you to be with me.

FABIAN
Forever?

BUTCH
...and ever.

Fabian lies her head back.

Butch continues to massage her crotch.

FABIAN
Do you love me?

BUTCH
Oui.

FABIAN
Butch? Will you give me oral pleasure?

Butch kisses her on the mouth.

BUTCH
Will you kiss it?

She nods her head: "yes."

FABIAN
But you first.

Butch's head goes down out of frame to carry out the oral pleasure. Fabian's face is alone in the frame.

FABIAN
(in French, with English subtitles)
Butch my love, the adventure begins.

FADE TO BLACK

FADE UP:

45. MOTEL ROOM 45.

Same motel room, except empty. WE HEAR THE SHOWER RUNNING in the bathroom. The CAMERA MOVES to the bathroom doorway. We see Fabian in a white terry cloth robe that seems to swallow her up. She's drying her head with a towel. Butch is inside the shower washing up. We see the outline of his naked body through the smoky glass of the shower door. Steam fills the bathroom. Butch turns the shower off and opens the door, popping his head out.

BUTCH
I think I cracked a rib.

FABIAN
Giving me oral pleasure?

BUTCH
No retard, from the fight.

FABIAN
Don't call me retard.

BUTCH
(in a Mongoloid voice)
My name is Fabby! My name is Fabby!

FABIAN
Shut up fuck head! I hate that Mongoloid voice.

BUTCH
Okay, sorry, sorry, sorry, I take it back! Can I have a towel please, Miss Beautiful Tulip.

FABIAN
Oh I like that, I like being called a tulip. Tulip is much better than Mongoloid.

She finishes drying her hair and wraps the towel like a turban on her head.

BUTCH
I didn't call you a Mongoloid, I called you a retard, but I took it back.

She hands him a towel.

BUTCH
Merci beaucoup.

FABIAN
Butch?

BUTCH
(drying his head)
Yes, lemon pie.

FABIAN
Where are we going to go?

BUTCH
I'm not sure yet. Wherever you want. We're gonna get a lot of money from this. But it ain't gonna be so much, we can live like hogs in the fat house forever. I was thinking we could go somewhere in the South Pacific. The kinda money we'll have'll carry us a long way down there.

FABIAN
So if we wanted, we could live in Bora Bora?

BUTCH
You betcha. And if after awhile you don't dig Bora Bora, then we can move over to Tahiti or Mexico.

FABIAN
But I do not speak Spanish.

BUTCH
You don't speak Bora Boran either. Besides, Mexican is easy: Donde esta el zapataria?

FABIAN
What does that mean?

BUTCH
Where's the shoe store?

FABIAN
Donde esta el zapataria?

BUTCH
Excellent pronunciation. You'll be my little mama cita in no time.

Butch exits the bathroom. We stay on Fabian as she brushes her teeth.

Butch keeps on from the other room.

BUTCH (OS)
Que hora es?

FABIAN
Que hora es?

BUTCH (OS)
What time is it?

FABIAN
What time is it?

BUTCH (OS)
Time for bed. Sweet dreams, jellybean.

Fabian brushes her teeth. We watch her for a moment or two, then she remembers something.

FABIAN
Butch.

She walks out of the bathroom to ask Butch a question, only to find him sound asleep in bed.

She looks at him a moment.

FABIAN
Forget it.

She exits frame, going back in the bathroom. WE STAY on the WIDE SHOT of the unconscious Butch in bed.

FADE TO BLACK

FADE UP:

46. MOTEL ROOM – MORNING 46.

SAME SHOT AS BEFORE, the next morning. We find Butch still asleep in bed.

Fabian brushes her teeth half in and half out of the bathroom so she can watch TV at the same time. She still wears the terry cloth robe from the night before.

ON TV: WILLIAM SMITH and a bunch of Hell's Angels are taking on the entire Vietnamese army in the film "THE LOSERS."

Butch wakes from his sleep, as if a scary monster was chasing him. His start startles Fabian.

FABIAN
Merde! You startled me. Did you have a bad dream?

Butch squints down the front of the bed at her, trying to focus.

BUTCH
...yeah...are you still brushing your teeth?

FABIAN
This is me. I brush my teeth all night long and into the early morning. Do you think I have a problem?

Fabian goes back into the bathroom to spit.

If that was supposed to be sarcasm, it was lost on Butch at this early hour.

Butch, still trying to chase the cobwebs away, sees on TV Hell's Angels tear-assin' through a Vietnamese prison camp.

BUTCH
What are you watching?

FABIAN (OS)
A motorcycle movie, I'm not sure the name.

BUTCH
Are you watchin' it?

Fabian reenters the room.

FABIAN
In a way. Why? Would you like for me to switch it off?

BUTCH
Would you please?

She reaches over and turns off the TV.

BUTCH
It's a little too early in the morning for explosions and war.

FABIAN
What was it about?

BUTCH
How should I know, you were the one watchin' it.

Fabian laughs.

FABIAN
No, imbecile, what was your dream about?

BUTCH
Oh, I...don't remember. It's really rare I remember a dream.

FABIAN
You just woke up from it.

BUTCH
Fabian, I'm not lying to you, I don't remember.

FABIAN
Well, let's look at the grumpy man in the morning. I didn't say you were lying, it's just odd you don't remember your dreams. I always remember mine. Did you know you talk in your sleep?

BUTCH
I don't talk in my sleep, do I talk in my sleep?

FABIAN
You did last night.

BUTCH
What did I say?

Lying on top of him.

FABIAN
I don't know. I couldn't understand you.

She kisses Butch.

FABIAN
Why don't you get up and we'll get some breakfast at that breakfast place with the pancakes.

BUTCH
One more kiss and I'll get up.

Fabian gives Butch a sweet long kiss.

FABIAN
Satisfied?

BUTCH
Yep.

FABIAN
Then get up, lazy bones.

Butch climbs out of bed and starts pulling clothes out of the suitcase that Fabian brought.

BUTCH
What time is it?

FABIAN
Almost nine in the morning. What time does our train arrive?

BUTCH
Eleven.

Seeing him looking at a pair of pants.

FABIAN
Those pants are very nice. Can you wear those with that nice blue shirt you have?

He pulls a blue shirt out of the suitcase.

BUTCH
This one?

FABIAN
That's the one. That matches.

BUTCH
Okay.

He puts the clothes on.

FABIAN
I'm gonna order a big plate of blueberry pancakes with maple syrup, eggs over easy, and five sausages.

BUTCH
(surprised at her potential appetite)
Anything to drink with that?

Butch is finished dressing.

FABIAN
(referring to his clothes)
Oh yes, that looks nice. To drink, a tall glass of orange juice and a black cup of coffee. After that, I'm going to have a slice of pie.

As he goes through the suitcases.

BUTCH
Pie for breakfast?

FABIAN
Any time of the day is a good time for pie. Blueberry pie to go with the pancakes. And on top, a thin slice of melted cheese --

BUTCH
-- where's my watch?

FABIAN
It's there.

BUTCH
No, it's not. It's not here.

FABIAN
Have you looked?

By now, Butch is frantically rummaging through the suitcases.

BUTCH
Yes I've fuckin' looked!!

He's now throwing clothes.

BUTCH
What the fuck do you think I'm doing?! Are you sure you got it?

Fabian can hardly speak, she's never seen Butch this way.

FABIAN
Uhhh...yes...beside the table drawer --

BUTCH
-- on the little kangaroo.

FABIAN
Yes, it was on your little kangaroo.

BUTCH
Well it's not here!

FABIAN
(on the verge of tears)
Well it should be!

BUTCH
Oh it most definitely should be here, but it's not. So where is it?

Fabian is crying and scared.

Butch lowers his voice, which only serves to make him more menacing.

BUTCH
Fabian, that was my father's fuckin' watch. You know what my father went through to git me that watch?...I don't wanna get into it right now...but he went through a lot. Now all this other shit, you coulda set on fire, but I specifically reminded you not to forget my father's watch. Now think, did you get it?

FABIAN
I believe so....

BUTCH
You believe so? You either did, or you didn't, now which one is it?

FABIAN
Then I did.

BUTCH
Are you sure?

FABIAN
(shaking)
No.

Butch freaks out, he punches the air.

Fabian SCREAMS and backs into a corner.

Butch picks up the motel TV and THROWS IT AGAINST the wall.

Fabian SCREAMS IN HORROR.

Butch looks toward her, suddenly calm.

BUTCH
(to Fabian)
No! It's not your fault.
(he approaches her)
You left it at the apartment.

He bends down in front of the woman who has sunk to the floor.

He touches her hand, she flinches.

BUTCH
If you did leave it at the apartment, it's not your fault. I had you bring a bunch of stuff. I reminded you about it, but I didn't illustrate how personal the watch was to me. If all I gave a fuck about was my watch, I should've told you. You ain't a mind reader.

He kisses her hand. Then rises.

Fabian is still sniffling.

Butch goes to the closet.

FABIAN
I'm sorry.

Butch puts on his high school jacket.

BUTCH
Don't be. It just means I won't be able to eat breakfast with you.

FABIAN
Why does it mean that?

BUTCH
Because I'm going back to my apartment to get my watch.

FABIAN
Won't the gangsters be looking for you there?

BUTCH
That's what I'm gonna find out. If they are, and I don't think I can handle it, I'll split.

Rising from the floor.

FABIAN
My darling, I don't want you to be murdered over a silly watch.

BUTCH
One, it's not a silly watch. Two, I'm not gonna be murdered. And three, don't be scared. I won't let anything get in the way of us living a happy life together.

FABIAN
What about our train?

BUTCH
We gotta couple hours yet.

FABIAN
I feel so dreadful. I saw your watch, I thought I brought it. I'm so sorry.

Butch brings her close and puts his hands on her face.

BUTCH
Don't feel bad, sugar pop. Nothing you could ever do would make me permanently angry at you.
(pause)
I love you, remember?
(he digs some money out of his wallet)
Now here's some money, order those pancakes and have a great breakfast.

FABIAN
Don't go.

BUTCH
I'll be back before you can say, blueberry pie.

FABIAN
Blueberry pie.

BUTCH
Well maybe not that fast, but fast.
Okay? Okay?

FABIAN
Okay.

He kisses her once more and heads for the door.

BUTCH
Bye-bye, sugar pop.

FABIAN
Bye.

BUTCH
I'm gonna take your Honda.

FABIAN
Okay.

And with that, he's out the door.

Fabian sits on the bed and looks at the money he gave her.

47. INT. HONDA (MOVING) – DAY 47.

Butch is beating the steering wheel and the dash with his fists as he drives down the street.

BUTCH
Of all the fuckin' things she
coulda forgot, she forgets my
father's watch. I specifically
reminded her not to forget it.
"Bedside table -- on the kangaroo."
I said the words: "Don't forget my
father's watch."

48. EXT. CITY STREET – DAY 48.

The little Honda races toward its destination as fast as its little engine will take it.

49. INT. HONDA (MOVING) – DAY 49.

Butch continues:

BUTCH
What the fuck am I doin'? Have I taken one too many hits to the head? That's gotta be it. Brain damage is the only excuse for this dumb a move. Stop the car, Butch.
(he keeps on driving)
Stop the car, Butch.
(he pays no attention to himself)
Butch, I'm talkin' to you. Put-your-foot-on-the-brake!

Butch's foot SLAMS down hard on the brake.

50. EXT. CITY STREET – DAY 50.

The little Honda SKIDS to a stop in the middle of the street. Butch HOPS out of the car like it was on fire.

Butch begins PACING back and forth, talking to himself, oblivious to PASSERSBY and traffic.

BUTCH
I ain't gonna do this. This is a punchy move and I ain't punchy! Daddy would totally fuckin' understand. If he was here right now, he'd say, "Butch, git a grip. It's a fuckin' watch, man. You lose one, ya git another. This is your life you're fuckin' around with, which you shouldn't be doin' 'cause you only got one.

Butch continues to pace, but now he's silent. Then....

BUTCH
This is my war. You see, Butch, what you're forgettin' is this watch isn't just a device that enables you to keep track of time. This watch is a symbol. It's a symbol of how your father, and his father before him, and his father before him, distinguished themselves in war. And when I took Marsellus Wallace's money, I started a war. This is my World War Two. That apartment in North Hollywood, that's my Wake Island.
(MORE)

BUTCH (CONT'D)
In fact, if you look at it that way, it's almost kismet that Fabian left it behind. And using that perspective, going back for it isn't stupid. It may be dangerous, but it's not stupid. Because there are certain things in this world that are worth going back for.

That's it, Butch has talked himself into it again. He HOPS in the car, starts it up and TAKES OFF.

CUT TO:

A parking meter red flag rises up, then out, leaving the arrow pointing at one hour.

51. EXT. RESIDENTIAL STREET CORNER – DAY 51.

Butch isn't completely reckless. He has parked his car a couple of blocks from his apartment to check things out before he goes boppin' through the front door.

52. EXT. ALLEY – DAY 52.

Butch walks down the alley until he gets to another street, then he discreetly glances out.

53. EXT. STREET – BUTCH'S APARTMENT – DAY 53.

Everything seems normal. More or less the right number of cars on the street. None of the parked cars appear out of place. None of them have a couple of goons sitting inside. Basically, it looks like normal morning activity in front of Butch's home.

Butch peers around a wall, taking in the vital information.

BUTCH
(to himself)
Everything looks hunky dorie. Looks can be deceiving, but this time I don't think they are. Why waste the manpower to stake out my place. I'd have to be a fuckin' idiot to come back here. That's how you're gonna beat 'em Butch, they keep underestimating you.

Butch walks out of the alley and is ready for anything. He crosses the street and enters his apartment courtyard.

Across the street from Butch's building, on the corner, is a combination donut shop and Japanese restaurant. A big sign sticks up in the air, with the name "Teriyaki Donut" and a graphic of a donut sticking out of a bowl of rice.

54. EXT. BUTCH'S APARTMENT COURTYARD – DAY 54.

Butch is in the courtyard of his North Hollywood apartment building. Once again, everything appears normal -- the laundry room, the pool, his apartment door -- nothing appears disturbed.

Butch climbs the stairs leading to his apartment, number 12. He steps outside the door and listens inside. Nothing.

Butch slowly inserts the key into the door, quietly opening it.

55. INT. BUTCH'S APARTMENT – DAY 55.

His apartment hasn't been touched.

He cautiously steps inside, shuts the door and takes a quick look around. Obviously, no one is there.

Butch walks into his modest kitchen, and opens the refrigerator. He takes out a carton of milk and drinks from it.

With carton in hand, Butch surveys the apartment. Then he goes to the bedroom.

His bedroom is like the rest of the apartment -- neat, clean and anonymous. The only things personal in his room are a few boxing trophies, an Olympic silver medal, a framed issue of "Ring Magazine" with Butch on the cover, and a poster of Jerry Quarry and one of George Chuvalo.

Sure enough, there's the watch just like he said it was: on the bedside table, hanging on his little kangaroo statue.

He puts the milk down on the table, takes the watch, checks the time and puts it on. Smiling, Butch grabs the milk and exits the bedroom.

He walks through the apartment and back into the kitchen. He opens a cupboard and takes out a box of Pop Tarts. Putting down the milk, he opens the box, takes out two Pop Tarts and puts them in the toaster.

Butch glances to his right, his eyes fall on something.

What he sees is a small compact Czech M61 submachine gun with a huge silencer on it, lying on his kitchen counter.

BUTCH
(softly)
Holy shit.

He picks up the intimidating peace of weaponry and examines it.

Then...a toilet FLUSHES.

Butch looks up to the bathroom door, which is parallel to the kitchen. There is someone behind it.

Like a rabbit caught in a radish patch, Butch freezes, not knowing what to do.

The bathroom door opens and Vincent Vega steps out of the bathroom, tightening his belt. In his hand is the book "MODESTY BLAISE" by Peter O'Donnell.

Vincent and Butch lock eyes.

Vincent freezes.

Butch doesn't move, except to point the M61 in Vincent's direction.

Neither man opens his mouth.

Then...the toaster LOUDLY kicks up the Pop Tarts.

That's all the situation needed.

Butch's finger HITS the trigger.

MUFFLED FIRE SHOOTS out of the end of the gun.

Vincent is seemingly RACKED with twenty bullets SIMULTANEOUSLY -- LIFTING him off his feet, PROPELLING him through the air and CRASHING through the glass shower door at the end of the bathroom.

By the time Butch removes his finger from the trigger, Vincent is annihilated.

Butch stands frozen, amazed at what just happened. His look goes from the grease spot in the bathroom that was once Vincent, down to the powerful piece of artillery in his grip.

With the respect it deserves, Butch carefully places the M61 back on the kitchen counter.

Then he exits the apartment, quickly.

56. EXT. APARTMENT COURTYARD – DAY 56.

Butch, not running, but walking very rapidly, crosses the courtyard....

...comes out of the apartment building, crosses the street....

...goes through the alley....

...and into his car in one STEADICAM SHOT.

57. EXT. HONDA – DAY 57.

Butch CRANKS the car into gear and drives away. The big wide smile of a survivor breaks across his face.

58. EXT. APARTMENT BUILDING STREET – DAY 58.

The Honda turns down the alley and slowly cruises by his apartment building.

59. INT. HONDA – DAY 59.

Butch looks out the window at his former home.

BUTCH
That's how you're gonna beat 'em, Butch. They keep underestimatin' ya.

This makes the boxer laugh out loud. As he laughs, he flips a tape in the cassette player. When the MUSIC starts, he SINGS along with it.

He drives by the apartment, but is stopped at the light on the corner across from Teriyaki Donut.

Butch is still chuckling, singing along with the song, as we see:

THROUGH THE WINDSHIELD
the big man himself, Marsellus Wallace, exit Teriyaki Donut, carrying a box of a dozen donuts and two large styrofoam cups of coffee. He steps off the curb, crossing the street in

front of Butch's car. This is the first time we see Marsellus clearly.

Laughing boy stops when he sees the big man directly in front of him.

When Marsellus is in front of Butch's car, he casually glances to his left, sees Butch, continues walking...then STOPS!

DOUBLE-TAKE: "Am I really seeing what I'm seeing?"

Butch doesn't wait for the big man to answer his own question. He STOMPS on the gas pedal.

The little Honda SLAMS into Marsellus, sending him, the donuts and the coffee HITTING the pavement at thirty miles an hour.

Butch CUTS into cross traffic and is BROAD-SIDED by a gold Camaro Z-28, BREAKING all the windows in the Honda and sending it up on the sidewalk.

Butch sits dazed and confused in the crumpled mess of what at one time was Fabian's Honda. Blood flows from his nostrils. The still-functional tape player continues to play. A PEDESTRIAN pokes his head inside.

PEDESTRIAN
Jesus, are you okay?

Butch looks at him, spaced-out.

BUTCH
I guess.

Marsellus Wallace lies sprawled out in the street. GAWKERS gather around the body.

GAWKER #1
(to the others)
He's dead! He's dead!

This jerk's yelling makes Marsellus come to.

TWO PEDESTRIANS help the shaken Butch out of the wreckage.

The woozy Marsellus gets to his feet.

GAWKER #2
If you need a witness in court, I'll be glad to help. He was a drunken maniac. He hit you and crashed into that car.

MARSELLUS
(still incoherent)
Who?

GAWKER #2
(pointing at Butch)
Him.

Marsellus follows the Gawker's finger and sees Butch Coolidge down the street, looking a shambles.

MARSELLUS
Well, I'll be damned.

The big man takes out a .45 Automatic and the Gawkers back away. Marsellus starts moving toward Butch.

Butch sees the fierce figure making a wobbly bee-line toward him.

BUTCH
Sacre bleu.

Marsellus brings up his weapon and FIRES, but he's so hurt, shaky and dazed that his arm goes wild.

He HITS a LOOKY-LOO WOMAN in the hip. She falls to the ground, screaming.

LOOKY-LOO WOMAN
Oh my god, I've been shot!

That's all Butch needs to see. He's outta there.

Marsellus RUNS after him.

The CROWD looks agape.

Butch is in a mad, limping RUN.

The big man's hot on his ass with a cockeyed wobbly run.

Butch cuts across traffic and dashes into a business with a sign that reads "MASON-DIXON PAWNSHOP."

60. INT. MASON-DIXON PAWNSHOP – DAY 60.

MAYNARD, a hillbilly-lookin' boy, stands behind the counter of his pawnshop when, all of a sudden, chaos in the form of Butch RACES into his world.

MAYNARD
Can I help you wit' somethin'?

BUTCH
Shut up!

Butch quickly takes measure of the situation, then stands next to the door.

MAYNARD
Now you just wait one goddamn minute --

Before Maynard can finish his threat, Marsellus CHARGES in. He doesn't get past the doorway because Butch LANDS his fist in Marsellus' face.

The gangster's feet go out from under him and the big man FALLS FLAT on his back.

Outside, two police cars with their SIRENS BLARING race by.

Butch POUNCES on the fallen body, PUNCHING him twice more in the face.

Butch takes the gun out of Marsellus' hand, then grabs ahold of his middle finger.

BUTCH
So you like chasing people, huh?

He BREAKS the finger. Marsellus lets out a pain sound. Butch then places the barrel of the .45 between his eyes, PULLS back the hammer and places his open hand behind the gun to shield the splatter.

BUTCH
Well guess what, big man, you caught me --

MAYNARD (OS)
-- hold it right there, godammit!

Butch and Marsellus look up at Maynard, who's brandishing a pump-action shotgun, aimed at the two men.

BUTCH
Look mister, this ain't any of your business --

MAYNARD
-- I'm makin' it my business! Now toss that gun!

Butch does.

MAYNARD

Now you on top, stand up and come to the counter.

Butch slowly gets up and moves to the counter. As soon as he gets there, Maynard HAULS OFF, HITTING him hard in the face with the butt of the shotgun, knocking Butch down and out.

After Butch goes down, Maynard calmly lays the shotgun on the counter and moves to the telephone.

Marsellus Wallace, from his position on the floor, groggily watches the pawnshop owner dial a number. Maynard waits on the line while the other end rings. Then it picks up.

MAYNARD

(into phone)

Zed? It's Maynard. The spider just caught a coupl'a flies.

Marsellus passes out.

FADE TO BLACK

FADE UP:

61. INT. PAWNSHOP BACK ROOM – DAY 61.

TWO SHOT -- BUTCH AND MARSELLUS
are tied up in two separate chairs. In their mouths are two S&M-style ball gags (a belt goes around their heads and a little red ball sticks in their mouths). Both men are unconscious. Maynard steps in with a fire extinguisher and SPRAYS both guys until they're wide awake and wet as otters. The two prisoners look up at their captor.

Maynard stands in front of them, fire extinguisher in one hand, shotgun in the other, and Marsellus' .45 sticking in his belt.

MAYNARD

Nobody kills anybody in my place of business except me or Zed.

A BUZZER buzzes.

MAYNARD

That's Zed.

Without saying another word, Maynard climbs up the stairs that lead to red curtains and goes through them.

WE HEAR, on the other side of the curtains, Maynard let Zed inside the store.

Butch and Marsellus look around the room. The basement of the pawnshop has been converted into a dungeon. After taking in their predicament, Butch and Marsellus look at each other, all traces of hostility gone, replaced by a terror they both share at what they've gotten themselves into.

Maynard and ZED come through the curtains. Zed is an even more intense version of Maynard, if such a thing is possible. The two hillbillys are obviously brothers. Where Maynard is a vicious pitbull, Zed is a deadly cobra. Zed walks in and stands in front of the two captives. He inspects them for a long time, then says:

ZED
(to Maynard)
You said you waited for me?

MAYNARD
I did.

ZED
Then how come they're all beat up?

MAYNARD
They did that to each other. They was fightin' when they came in. This one was gonna shoot that one.

ZED
(to Butch)
You were gonna shoot him?

Butch makes no reply.

ZED
Hey, is Grace gonna be okay in front of this place?

MAYNARD
Yeah, it ain't Tuesday is it?

ZED
No, it's Thursday.

MAYNARD
Then she'll be fine.

ZED
Bring out The Gimp.

MAYNARD
I think The Gimp's asleep.

ZED
Well, I guess you'll just wake 'em up then, won't you?

Maynard opens a trap door in the floor.

MAYNARD
(yelling in the hole)
Wake up!

Maynard reaches into the hole and comes back holding onto a leash. He gives it a rough yank and, from below the floor, rises THE GIMP.

The Gimp is a man they keep dressed from head to toe in black leather bondage gear. There are zippers, buckles and studs here and there on the body. On his head is a black leather mask with two eye holes and a zipper (closed) for a mouth. They keep him in a hole in the floor big enough for a large dog.

Zed takes the chair, sits it in front of the two prisoners, then lowers into it. Maynard hands The Gimp's leash to Zed, then backs away.

ZED
(to The Gimp)
Down!

The Gimp gets on its knees.

Maynard hangs back while Zed appraises the two men.

MAYNARD
Who's first?

ZED
I ain't fer sure yet.

Then with his little finger, Zed does a silent "Eenie, meany, miney, moe..." just his mouth mouthing the words and his finger going back and forth between the two.

Butch and Marsellus are terrified.

Maynard looks back and forth at the victims.

The Gimp's eyes go from one to the other inside the mask.

Zed continues his silent sing-song with his finger moving left to right, then it stops.

TWO SHOT -- BUTCH AND MARSELLUS
after a beat, THE CAMERA MOVES to the right, zeroing in on Marsellus.

Zed stands up.

ZED
Wanna do it here?

MAYNARD
Naw, drag big boy to Russell's old room.

Zed grabs Marsellus' chair and DRAGS him into Russell's old room. Russell, no doubt, was some other poor bastard that had the misfortune of stumbling into the Mason-Dixon pawnshop. Whatever happened to Russell is known only to Maynard and Zed because his old room, a back room in the back of the back room, is empty.

As Marsellus is dragged away, he locks eyes with Butch before he disappears behind the door of Russell's old room.

MAYNARD
(to The Gimp)
Up!

The Gimp rises. Maynard ties The Gimp's leash to a hook on the ceiling.

MAYNARD
Keep an eye on this one.

The Gimp bows its head: "yes." Maynard disappears into Russell's old room. There must be a stereo in there because suddenly The Judds, singing in harmony, fills the air.

Butch looks at The Gimp. The Gimp giggles from underneath the mask as if this were the funniest moment in the history of comedy.

From behind the door we hear country MUSIC, struggling, and:

MAYNARD (OS)
Whoa, this boy's got a bit of fight in 'em!

We the HEAR Maynard and Zed beat on Marsellus.

ZED (OS)
You wanna fight? You wanna fight? Good, I like to fight!

Butch pauses, listens to the voices. Then, in a panic, hurriedly struggles to get free.

The Gimp is laughing wildly.

The ropes are on too tight and Butch can't break free.

The Gimp slaps his knee laughing.

~~In the back room, we hear:~~

MAYNARD (OS)
That's it...that's it boy, you're goin' fine. Oooooooh, just like that...that's good.
(grunting faster)
Stay still...stay still goddamn ya! Zed goddammit, git over here and hold 'em!

Butch stops struggling and lifts up on his arms. Then, quite easily, the padded chair back slides up and off as if it were never connected by a bolt.

The Gimp sees this and its eyes widen.

THE GIMP
Huhng?

The Gimp FLAILS WILDLY, trying to get the leash off the hook. He tries to yell, but all that comes out are excited gurgles and grunts.

Butch is out of his chair, quickly dispensing three BOXER'S PUNCHES to its face. The punches knock The Gimp out, making him fall to his knees, thus HANGING HIMSELF by the leash attached to the hook.

Butch removes the ball gag, then silently makes his way through the red curtains.

62. INT. PAWNSHOP – DAY 62.

Butch sneaks to the door.

On the counter is a big set of keys with a large Z connected to the ring. Grabbing them, he's about to go out when he stops and listens to the hillbilly psychopaths having their way with Marsellus.

Butch decides for the life of him, he can't leave anybody in a situation like that. So he begins rooting around the pawnshop for a weapon to bash those hillbillies' heads in with.

He picks up a big destructive-looking hammer, then discards it: not destructive enough. He picks up a chainsaw, thinks about it for a moment, then puts it back. Next, a large Louisville slugger he tries on for size. But then he spots what he's been looking for:

A Samurai sword.

It hangs in its hand-carved wood sheath from a nail on the wall, next to a neon "DAD'S OLD-FASHIONED ROOT BEER" sign. Butch takes the sword off the wall, removing it from its sheath. It's a magnificent piece of steel. It seems to glisten in the low-wattage light of the pawnshop. Butch touches his thumb to the blade to see if the sword is just for show. Not on your life. It's as sharp as it gets. This weapon seems made to order for the Brothers Grimm downstairs. Holding the sword pointed downward, Takakura Ken-style, he disappears through the red curtains to take care of business.

63. INT. PAWNSHOP BACK ROOM – DAY 63.

Butch quietly sneaks down the stairs leading to the dungeon. Sodomy and the Judds can still be heard going strong behind the closed door that leads to Russell's old room.

64. INT. RUSSELL'S OLD ROOM – DAY 64.

Butch's hand comes into frame, pushing the door open. It swings open silently, revealing the rapists, who have switched
positions. Zed is now bent over Marsellus, who is bent over a wooden horse. Maynard watches. Both have their backs to Butch.

Maynard faces the CAMERA, grinning, while Butch comes up behind him with the sword.

Miserable, violated, and looking like a rag doll, Marsellus, red ball gag still in mouth, opens his watery eyes to see Butch coming up behind Maynard. His eyes widen.

BUTCH
Hey hillbilly.

Maynard turns and sees Butch holding the sword.

Butch SCREAMS...with one mighty SWING, SLASHES Maynard across his front, moving past him, eyes and blade now locked on Zed.

Maynard stands trembling, his front sliced open, in shock.

Butch, while never taking his eyes off Zed, THRUSTS the sword behind him, SKEWERING Maynard, then EXTRACTS it, pointing the blade toward Zed. Maynard COLLAPSES.

Zed disengages from Marsellus in a hurry and his eyes go from the tip of Butch's sword to Marsellus' .45 Automatic, which lies within reach.

Butch's eyes follow Zed's.

BUTCH
You want that gun, Zed? Pick it up.

Zed's hand inches toward the weapon.

Butch GRIPS the sword tighter.

Zed studies Butch.

Butch looks hard at Zed.

Then a VOICE says:

MARSELLUS (OS)
Step aside, Butch.

Butch steps aside, REVEALING Marsellus standing behind him, holding Maynard's pump-action shotgun.

KABOOM!!!!

Zed is BLASTED in the groin. Down he goes, SCREAMING in AGONY.

Marsellus, looking down at his whimpering rapist, EJECTS the used shotgun shell.

Butch lowers the sword and hangs back. Not a word, until:

BUTCH
You okay?

MARSELLUS
Naw man. I'm pretty fuckin' far from okay!

Long pause.

BUTCH
What now?

MARSELLUS
What now? Well let me tell you what now. I'm gonna call a coupla pipe-hittin' niggers, who'll go to work on homes here with a pair of pliers and a blow torch.
(to Zed)
Hear me talkin' hillbilly boy?! I ain't through with you by a damn sight. I'm gonna git Medieval on your ass.

BUTCH
I meant what now, between me and you?

MARSELLUS
Oh, that what now? Well, let me tell ya what now between me an' you. There is no me an' you. Not no more.

BUTCH
So we're cool?

MARSELLUS
Yeah man, we're cool. One thing I ask -- two things I ask: don't tell nobody about this. This shit's between me and you and the soon-to-be-livin'-the-rest-of-his-short-ass-life-in-agonizing-pain, Mr. Rapist here. It ain't nobody else's business. Two: leave town. Tonight. Right now. And when you're gone, stay gone. You've lost your Los Angeles privileges. Deal?

BUTCH
Deal.

The two men shake hands, then hug one another.

MARSELLUS
Go on now, get your ass outta here.

Butch leaves Russell's old room through the red curtains. Marsellus walks over to a phone, dialing a number.

MARSELLUS
(into the phone)
Hello Mr. Wolf, it's Marsellus. Gotta bit of a situation.

65. EXT. MASON-DIXON PAWNSHOP – DAY 65.

Butch, still shaking in his boots, exits the pawnshop. He looks ahead and sees, parked in front of the establishment, Zed's Big Chrome Chopper with a teardrop gas tank that has the name "GRACE" on it. He climbs aboard, takes out the keys with the big Z on them and starts up the huge hog. It RUMBLES to life, making sounds like a rocket fighting for orbit. Butch twists the accelerator handle and SPEEDS off.

WE CUT BACK AND FORTH BETWEEN...

66. INT. BUTCH AND FABIAN'S HOTEL ROOM – DAY 66.

Fabian stands in front of a mirror wearing a "Frankie says, Relax" tee-shirt, singing along with MUSIC coming from a BOOM BOX.

67. EXT. CITY STREET – CHOPPER (MOVING) – DAY 67.

Butch drives down the street, humping a hot hog named "GRACE."
He checks his father's watch. It says: 10:30.

The SONG in the motel room PLAYS OVER this.

68. EXT. MOTEL ROOM – DAY 68.

Butch rides up on Grace. He hops off and runs inside the motel room, while we stay outside with the bike.

FABIAN (OS)
Butch, I was so worried!

BUTCH
Honey, grab your radio and your purse and let's go!

FABIAN (OS)
But what about all our bags?

BUTCH
Fuck the bags. We'll miss our train if we don't split now.

FABIAN (OS)
Is everything well? Are we in danger?

BUTCH
We're cool. In fact, we're super-cool. But we gots ta go. I'll wait for you outside.

Butch runs out and hops back on the bike. Fabian exits the motel room with the boom box and a large purse. When she sees Butch on the chopper, she stops dead.

FABIAN
Where did you get this motorcycle?

BUTCH
(he KICKS-STARTS it)
It's a chopper, baby, hop on.

Fabian slowly approaches the two-wheel demon.

FABIAN
What happened to my Honda?

BUTCH
Sorry baby, I crashed your Honda.

FABIAN
You're hurt?

BUTCH
I might've broke my nose, no biggie. Hop on.

She doesn't move.

Butch looks at her.

BUTCH
Honey, we gotta hit the fuckin' road!

Fabian starts to cry.

Butch realizes that this is not the way to get her on the bike. He turns off the engine and reaches out, taking her hand.

BUTCH
I'm sorry, baby-love.

FABIAN
(crying)
You were gone so long, I started to think dreadful thoughts.

BUTCH
I'm sorry I worried you, sweetie. Everything's fine. Hey, how was breakfast?

FABIAN
(waterworks drying a little)
It was good --

BUTCH
-- did you get the blueberry pancakes?

FABIAN
No, they didn't have blueberry pancakes, I had to get buttermilk -- are you sure you're okay?

BUTCH
Baby-love, from the moment I left you, this has been without a doubt the single weirdest day of my entire life. Climb on an' I'll tell ya about it.

Fabian does climb on. Butch STARTS her up.

FABIAN
Butch, whose motorcycle is this?

BUTCH
It's a chopper.

FABIAN
Whose chopper is this?

BUTCH
Zed's.

FABIAN
Who's Zed?

BUTCH
Zed's dead, baby, Zed's dead.

And with that, the two lovebirds PEEL AWAY on Grace, as the SONG on the BOOM BOX RISES.

FADE TO BLACK

TITLE CARD:

"JULES
VINCENT
JIMMIE
&
THE WOLF"

TITLE DISAPPEARS.

Over black, we can HEAR in the distance, men talking.

JULES (OS)
You ever read the Bible, Brett?

BRETT (OS)
Yes!

JULES (OS)
There's a passage I got memorized, seems appropriate for this situation. Ezekiel 25:17. "The path of the righteous man is beset on all sides by the inequities of the selfish and the tyranny of evil men...."

FADE UP:

69. INT. BATHROOM – DAY 69.

We're in the bathroom of the Hollywood apartment we were in earlier. In fact, we're there at exactly the same time. Except this time, we're in the bathroom with the FOURTH MAN. The Fourth Man is pacing around the small room, listening hard to what's being said on the other side of the door, tightly CLUTCHING his huge silver .357 Magnum.

JULES (OS)
"...blessed is he who, in the name of charity and good will, shepherds the weak through the valley of darkness. And I will strike down upon thee with great vengeance and furious anger those who attempt to poison and destroy my brothers. And you will know I am the Lord when I lay my vengeance upon you."

BANG! BANG! BOOM! POW! BAM BAM BAM BAM BAM!

The Fourth Man freaks out. He THROWS himself against the back wall, gun outstretched in front of him, a look of yellow fear on his face, ready to blow in half anybody fool enough to stick their head through that door.

Then he listens to them talk.

VINCENT (OS)
Friend of yours?

JULES (OS)
Yeah, Marvin-Vincent-Vincent-Marvin.

Waiting for them isn't the smartest move. Bursting out the door and blowing them all away while they're fuckin' around is the way to go.

70. INT. APARTMENT — DAY 70.

The bathroom door BURSTS OPEN and the Fourth Man CHARGES out, silver Magnum raised, FIRING SIX BOOMING SHOTS from his hand cannon.

FOURTH MAN
Die...die...die...die...!

DOLLY INTO Fourth Man, same as before.

He SCREAMS until he's dry firing. Then, a look of confusion crosses his face.

TWO SHOT -- JULES AND VINCENT
standing next to each other, unharmed. Amazing as it seems, none of the Fourth Man's shots appear to have hit anybody. Jules and Vincent exchange looks like, "Are we hit?" They're as confused as the shooter. After looking at each other, they bring their looks up to the Fourth Man.

FOURTH MAN
I don't understand --

The Fourth Man is taken out of the scenario by the two men's bullets who, unlike his, HIT their marks. He drops DEAD.

The two men lower their guns. Jules, obviously shaken, sits down in a chair. Vincent, after a moment of respect, shrugs it off. Then heads toward Marvin in the corner.

VINCENT
Why the fuck didn't you tell us about that guy in the bathroom? Slip your mind? Forget he was in there with a goddamn hand cannon?

JULES
(to himself)
We should be fuckin' dead right now.
(pause)
Did you see that gun he fired at us? It was bigger than him.

VINCENT
.357.

JULES
We should be fuckin' dead!

VINCENT
Yeah, we were lucky.

Jules rises, moving toward Vincent.

JULES
That shit wasn't luck. That shit was somethin' else.

Vincent prepares to leave.

VINCENT
Yeah, maybe.

JULES
That was...divine intervention. You know what divine intervention is?

VINCENT
Yeah, I think so. That means God came down from Heaven and stopped the bullets.

JULES
Yeah man, that's what it means. That's exactly what it means! God came down from Heaven and stopped the bullets.

VINCENT
I think we should be going now.

JULES
Don't do that! Don't you fuckin' do that! Don't blow this shit off! What just happened was a fuckin' miracle!

VINCENT
Chill the fuck out, Jules, this shit happens.

JULES
Wrong, wrong, this shit doesn't just happen.

VINCENT
Do you wanna continue this theological discussion in the car, or at the jailhouse with the cops?

JULES
We should be fuckin' dead now, my friend! We just witnessed a miracle, and I want you to fuckin' acknowledge it!

VINCENT
Okay man, it was a miracle, can we leave now?

71. EXT. HOLLYWOOD APARTMENT BUILDING – MORNING 71.

The Chevy Nova PROPELS itself into traffic.

72. INT. NOVA (MOVING) – MORNING 72.

Jules is behind the wheel, Vincent in the passenger seat and Marvin in the back.

VINCENT
...ever seen that show "COPS?" I was watchin' it once and this cop was on it who was talkin' about this time he got into this gun fight with a guy in a hallway. He unloads on this guy and he doesn't hit anything. And these guys were in a hallway. It's a freak, but it happens.

JULES
If you wanna play blind man, then go walk with a Shepherd. But me, my eyes are wide fuckin' open.

VINCENT
What the fuck does that mean?

JULES
That's it for me. From here on in, you can consider my ass retired.

VINCENT
Jesus Christ!

JULES
Don't blaspheme!

VINCENT
Goddammit, Jules --

JULES
-- I said don't do that --

VINCENT
-- you're fuckin' freakin' out!

JULES
I'm tellin' Marsellus today I'm through.

VINCENT
While you're at it, be sure to tell 'im why.

JULES
Don't worry, I will.

VINCENT
I'll bet ya ten thousand dollars, he laughs his ass off.

JULES
I don't give a damn if he does.

Vincent turns to the backseat with the .45 casually in his grip.

VINCENT
Marvin, what do you make of all this?

MARVIN
I don't even have an opinion.

VINCENT
C'mon, Marvin. Do you think God came down from Heaven and stopped the bullets?

Vincent's .45 goes BANG!

Marvin is hit in the upper chest, below the throat. He GURGLES blood and SHAKES.

JULES
What the fuck's happening?

VINCENT
I just accidentally shot Marvin in the throat.

JULES
Why the fuck did you do that?

VINCENT
I didn't mean to do it. I said it was an accident.

JULES
I've seen a lot of crazy-ass shit in my time --

VINCENT
-- chill out, man, it was an accident, okay? You hit a bump or somethin' and the gun went off.

JULES
The car didn't hit no motherfuckin' bump!

VINCENT
Look! I didn't mean to shoot this son-of-a-bitch, the gun just went off, don't ask me how! Now I think the humane thing to do is put him out of his misery.

JULES
(can't believe it)
You wanna shoot 'im again?

VINCENT
The guy's sufferin'. It's the right thing to do.

Marvin, suffering though he is, is listening to this debate, not believing what he's hearing.

After a pause.

JULES
This is really uncool.

Vincent turns to the backseat, places the barrel of the .45 against Marvin's forehead. Marvin's eyes are as big as saucers. He tries to talk Vince out of this, but when he opens his mouth, only GURGLES come out.

JULES
Marvin, I just wanna apologize. I got nothin' to do with this shit. And I want you to know I think it's fucked up.

VINCENT
Okay, Pontius Pilot, when I count three, honk your horn. One... two...

CU of the steering wheel.

VINCENT (OS)
...three.

Jules presses down hard on the horn: HONK and BANG!

When we CUT BACK to the two men, the car is completely covered in blood. It's all over everything, including Jules and Vincent.

JULES
Jesus Christ Almighty!

VINCENT
(to himself)
Fuck.

JULES
Look at this mess! We're drivin' around on a city street in broad daylight --

VINCENT
-- I know, I know, I wasn't thinkin' about the splatter.

JULES
Well you better be thinkin' about it now, motherfucker! We gotta get this car off the road. Cops tend to notice shit like you're driving a car drenched in fuckin' blood.

VINCENT
Can't we just take it to a friendly place?

JULES
This is the Valley, Vincent. Marsellus don't got no friendly places in the Valley.

VINCENT
Well, don't look at me, this is your town, Jules.

Jules takes out a cellular phone and starts punching digits.

VINCENT
Who ya callin'?

JULES
A buddy of mine in Toluca Lake.

VINCENT
Where's Toluca Lake?

JULES
On the other side of the hill, by Burbank Studios. If Jimmie's ass ain't home, I don't know what the fuck we're gonna do. I ain't got any other partners in 818.
(into phone)
Jimmie! How ya doin' man, it's Jules.
(pause)
Listen up man, me an' my homeboy are in some serious shit. We're in a car we gotta get off the road, pronto! I need to use your garage for a coupla hours.
(pause)
Jimmie, you know I can't get into this shit on a cellular fuckin' phone. But what I can say is my ass is out in the cold and I'm askin' you for some sanctuary 'til our people can bring us in.
(pause)
I appreciate this, man --
(pause)
We'll be gone by then.
(pause)
-- Jimmie, I'm aware of your situation. I ain't gonna fuck things up for you. I give you my word, partner, she'll never know we were there.
(pause)
Five minutes. Later.

He folds up the phone, turns to Vincent.

JULES
We're set. But his wife come home from work in an hour and a half and we gotta be outta there by then.

73. EXT. JIMMIE'S HOUSE – MORNING 73.

The Nova pulls into the garage of a two-bedroom suburban house.

74. INT. JIMMIE'S BATHROOM – DAY 74.

Jules is bent over a sink, washing his bloody hands while Vincent stands behind him.

JULES
We gotta be real fuckin' delicate with this Jimmie's situation. He's one remark away from kickin' our asses out the door.

VINCENT
If he kicks us out, whadda we do?

JULES
Well, we ain't leavin' 'til we made a coupla phone calls. But I never want it to reach that pitch. Jimmie's my friend and you don't bust in your friend's house and start tellin' 'im what's what.

Jules rises and dries his hands. Vincent takes his place at the sink.

VINCENT
Just tell 'im not to be abusive. He kinda freaked out back there when he saw Marvin.

JULES
Put yourself in his position. It's eight o'clock in the morning. He just woke up, he wasn't prepared for this shit. Don't forget who's doin' who a favor.

Vincent finishes, then dries his hands on a white towel.

VINCENT
If the price of that favor is I gotta take shit, he can stick his favor straight up his ass.

When Vincent is finished drying his hands, the towel is stained with red.

JULES
What the fuck did you just do to his towel?

VINCENT
I was just dryin' my hands.

JULES
You're supposed to wash 'em first.

VINCENT
You watched me wash 'em.

JULES
I watched you get 'em wet.

VINCENT
I washed 'em. Blood's real hard to get off. Maybe if he had some Lava, I coulda done a better job.

JULES
I used the same soap you did and when I dried my hands, the towel didn't look like a fuckin' Maxie pad. Look, fuck it, alright. Who cares? But it's shit like this that's gonna bring this situation to a boil. If he were to come in here and see that towel like that...I'm tellin' you Vincent, you best be cool. 'Cause if I gotta get in to it with Jimmie on account of you....Look, I ain't threatenin' you, I respect you an' all, just don't put me in that position.

VINCENT
Jules, you ask me nice like that, no problem. He's your friend, you handle him.

75. INT. JIMMIE'S KITCHEN – MORNING 75.

Three men are standing in Jimmie's kitchen, each with a mug of coffee. Jules, Vincent and JIMMIE DIMMICK, a young man in his late-20s dressed in a bathrobe.

JULES
Goddamn Jimmie, this is some serious gourmet shit. Me an' Vincent woulda been satisfied with freeze-dried Tasters Choice. You spring this gourmet fuckin' shit on us. What flavor is this?

JIMMIE
Knock it off, Julie.

JULES
What?

JIMMIE
I'm not a cob of corn, so you can stop butterin' me up. I don't need you to tell me how good my coffee is. I'm the one who buys it, I know how fuckin' good it is. When Bonnie goes shoppin', she buys shit. I buy the gourmet expensive stuff 'cause when I drink it, I wanna taste it. But what's on my mind at this moment isn't the coffee in my kitchen, it's the dead nigger in my garage.

JULES
Jimmie --

JIMMIE
-- I'm talkin'. Now let me ask you a question, Jules. When you drove in here, did you notice a sign out front that said, "Dead nigger storage?"

Jules starts to "Jimmie" him --

JIMMIE
-- answer to question. Did you see a sign out in front of my house that said, "Dead nigger storage?"

JULES
(playing along)
Naw man, I didn't.

JIMMIE
You know why you didn't see that sign?

JULES
Why?

JIMMIE
'Cause storin' dead niggers ain't my fuckin' business!

Jules starts to "Jimmie" him.

JIMMIE
-- I ain't through! Now don't you understand that if Bonnie comes home and finds a dead body in her house, I'm gonna get divorced. No marriage counselor, no trial separation -- fuckin' divorced. And I don't wanna get fuckin' divorced. The last time me an' Bonnie talked about this shit was gonna be the last time me an' Bonnie talked about this shit. Now I wanna help ya out Julie, I really do. But I ain't gonna lose my wife doin' it.

JULES
Jimmie --

JIMMIE
-- don't fuckin' Jimmie me, man, I can't be Jimmied. There's nothin' you can say that's gonna make me forget I love my wife. Now she's workin' the graveyard shift at the hospital. She'll be comin' home in less than an hour and a half. Make your phone calls, talk to your people, then get the fuck out of my house.

JULES
That's all we want. We don't wanna fuck up your shit. We just need to call our people to bring us in.

JIMMIE
Then I suggest you get to it. Phone's in my bedroom.

As Jules crosses the room, exiting.

JULES
(calling behind him)
You're a friend, Jimmie, you're a good fuckin' friend!

JIMMIE
(to himself)
Yeah, yeah, yeah, yeah, yeah. I'm a real good friend. Good friend, bad husband, soon to be ex-husband.
(looks up and sees Vincent)
Who the fuck are you?

VINCENT
I'm Vincent. And Jimmie, thanks a bunch.

The two men laugh.

JIMMIE
Don't mention it.

76. INT. MARSELLUS WALLACE'S DINING ROOM – MORNING 76.

Marsellus Wallace sits at his dining table in a big comfy robe, eating his large breakfast, while talking on the phone.

MARSELLUS
...well, say she comes home. Whaddya think she'll do?
(pause)
No fuckin' shit she'll freak. That ain't no kinda answer. You know 'er, I don't. How bad, a lot or a little?

77. INT. JIMMIE'S BEDROOM – MORNING 77.

Jules paces around in Jimmie's bedroom on the phone.

JULES
You got to appreciate what an explosive element this Bonnie situation is. If she comes home from a hard day's work and finds a bunch of gangsters doin' a bunch of gangsta' shit in her kitchen, ain't no tellin' what she's apt to do.

MARSELLUS
Let us speak of the unspeakable.

JULES
Possibility exists, but unlikely.

MARSELLUS
Why possible but unlikely?

JULES
'Cause if push met shove, you know I'll take care of business. But push ain't never gonna meet shove. Because you're gonna solve this shit fer us. You're gonna take our asses outta the cold and bring it inside where it's warm. 'Cause if I gotta get into it with my friend about his wife over your boy Vincent, I'm gonna have bad feelings.

MARSELLUS
I've grasped that, Jules. All I'm doin' is contemplating the "ifs."

JULES
I don't wanna hear about no motherfuckin' "ifs." What I wanna hear from your ass is: "you ain't got no problems, Jules. I'm on the motherfucker. Go back in there, chill them niggers out and wait for the cavalry, which should be comin' directly."

MARSELLUS
You ain't got no problems, Jules. I'm on the motherfucker. Go back in there, chill them niggers out and wait for The Wolf, who should be comin' directly.

JULES
You sendin' The Wolf?

MARSELLUS
Feel better?

JULES
Shit Negro, that's all you had to say.

78. INT. HOTEL SUITE – MORNING 78.

The CAMERA looks through the bedroom doorway of a hotel suite into the main area. We SEE a crap game being played on a fancy crap table by GAMBLERS in tuxedos and LUCKY LADIES in fancy evening gowns. The CAMERA PANS to the right revealing: sitting on a bed, phone in hand with his back to us, the tuxedo-clad WINSTON WOLF aka "THE WOLF."

We also see The Wolf has a small notepad that he jots details in.

THE WOLF
(into phone)
Is she the hysterical type?
(pause)
When she due?
(jotting down)
Give me the principals' names again?
(jots down)
Jules....

We SEE his book. The page has written on it:

1265 Riverside Drive
Toluca Lake
1 body (no head)
Bloody shot-up car
Jules (black)

THE WOLF
...Vincent...Jimmie...Bonnie....

He writes:

Vincent (Dean Martin)
Jimmie (house)
Bonnie (9:30)

THE WOLF
Expect a call around 10:30. It's about thirty minutes away. I'll be there in ten.

He hangs up. We never see his face.

CUT TO:

TITLE CARD OVER BLACK:
"NINE MINUTES AND THIRTY-SEVEN SECONDS LATER"

CUT TO:

79. EXT. JIMMIE'S STREET – MORNING 79.

A silver Porsche WHIPS the corner leading to Jimmie's home, in HYPER DRIVE. Easily doing 135 mph, the Porsche stops on a dime in front of Jimmie's house.

A ringed finger touches the doorbell: DING DONG.

80. INT. JIMMIE'S HOUSE – MORNING 80.

Jimmie opens the door. We see, standing in the doorway, the tuxedo-clad man. He looks down to his notebook, then up at Jimmie.

THE WOLF
You're Jimmie, right? This is your house?

JIMMIE
Yeah.

THE WOLF
(sticks his hand out)
I'm Winston Wolf, I solve problems.

JIMMIE
Good, 'cause we got one.

THE WOLF
So I heard. May I come in?

JIMMIE
Please do.

The two men walk to the dining room.

THE WOLF
I want to convey Mr. Wallace's gratitude with the help you're providing on this matter. Let me assure you Jimmie, Mr. Wallace's gratitude is worth having.

In the dining room, Jules and Vincent stand up.

THE WOLF
You must be Jules, which would make you Vincent. Let's get down to brass tacks, gentlemen. If I was informed correctly, the clock is ticking, is that right, Jimmie?

JIMMIE
100 percent.

THE WOLF
Your wife, Bonnie...
(refers to his pad)
...comes home at 9:30 in the AM, is that correct?

JIMMIE
Uh-huh.

THE WOLF
I was led to believe if she comes home and finds us here, she wouldn't appreciate it none too much.

JIMMIE
She won't at that.

THE WOLF
That gives us forty minutes to get the fuck outta Dodge, which, if you do what I say when I say it, should be plenty. Now you got a corpse in a car, minus a head, in a garage. Take me to it.

81. INT. JIMMIE'S GARAGE – MORNING 81.

The three men hang back as The Wolf examines the car. He studies the car in silence, opening the door, looking inside, circling it.

THE WOLF
Jimmie?

JIMMIE
Yes.

THE WOLF
Do me a favor, will ya? Thought I smelled some coffee in there. Would you make me a cup?

JIMMIE
Sure, how do you take it?

THE WOLF
Lotsa cream, lotsa sugar.

Jimmie exits. The Wolf continues his examination.

THE WOLF
About the car, is there anything I need to know? Does it stall, does it make a lot of noise, does it smoke, is there gas in it, anything?

JULES
Aside from how it looks, the car's cool.

THE WOLF
Positive? Don't get me out on the road and I find out the brake lights don't work.

JULES
Hey man, as far as I know, the motherfucker's tip-top.

THE WOLF
Good enough, let's go back to the kitchen.

82. INT. KITCHEN – MORNING 82.

Jimmie hands The Wolf a cup of coffee.

THE WOLF
Thank you, Jimmie.

He takes a sip, then, pacing as he thinks, lays out for the three men the plan of action.

THE WOLF
Okay first thing, you two.
(meaning Jules and Vincent)
Take the body, stick it in the trunk. Now Jimmie, this looks to be a pretty domesticated house. That would lead me to believe that in the garage or under the sink, you got a bunch of cleaners and cleansers and shit like that, am I correct?

JIMMIE
Yeah. Exactly. Under the sink.

THE WOLF

Good. What I need you two fellas to do is take those cleaning products and clean the inside of the car. And I'm talkin' fast, fast, fast. You need to go in the backseat, scoop up all those little pieces of brain and skull. Get it out of there. Wipe down the upholstery -- now when it comes to upholstery, it don't need to be spic and span, you don't need to eat off it. Give it a good once over. What you need to take care of are the really messy parts. The pools of blood that have collected, you gotta soak that shit up. But the windows are a different story. Them you really clean. Get the Windex, do a good job. Now Jimmie, we need to raid your linen closet. I need blankets, I need comforters, I need quilts, I need bedspreads. The thicker the better, the darker the better. No whites, can't use 'em. We need to camouflage the interior of the car. We're gonna line the front seat and the backseat and the floor boards with quilts and blankets. If a cop stops us and starts stickin' his big snout in the car, the subterfuge won't last. But at a glance, the car will appear to be normal. Jimmie -- lead the way, boys -- get to work.

The Wolf and Jimmie turn, heading for the bedroom, leaving Vincent and Jules standing in the kitchen.

VINCENT

(calling after him)

A "please" would be nice.

The Wolf stops and turns around.

THE WOLF

Come again?

VINCENT

I said a "please" would be nice.

The Wolf takes a step toward him.

THE WOLF

Get it straight, Buster. I'm not here to say "please." I'm here to tell you what to do. And if self-preservation is an instinct you possess, you better fuckin' do it and do it quick. I'm here to help. If my help's not appreciated, lotsa luck gentlemen.

JULES

It ain't that way, Mr. Wolf. Your help is definitely appreciated.

VINCENT

I don't mean any disrespect. I just don't like people barkin' orders at me.

THE WOLF

If I'm curt with you, it's because time is a factor. I think fast, I talk fast, and I need you guys to act fast if you want to get out of this. So pretty please, with sugar on top, clean the fuckin' car.

83. INT. JIMMIE'S BEDROOM – MORNING 83.

Jimmie's gathering all the bedspreads, quilts and linen he has. The Wolf is on the phone.

THE WOLF

(into phone)

It's a 1974 Chevy Nova.

(pause)

White.

(pause)

Nothin', except for the mess inside.

(pause)

About twenty minutes.

(pause)

Nobody who'll be missed.

(pause)

You're a good man, Joe. See ya soon.

(he looks to Jimmie)

How we comin', Jimmie?

Jimmie comes over with a handful of linen.

JIMMIE

Mr. Wolf, you gotta understand somethin' --

THE WOLF

-- Winston, Jimmie -- please, Winston.

JIMMIE

You gotta understand something, Winston. I want to help you guys out and all, but that's my best linen. It was a wedding present from my Uncle Conrad and Aunt Ginny, and they ain't with us anymore --

THE WOLF

-- let me ask you a question, if you don't mind?

JIMMIE

Sure.

THE WOLF

Were your Uncle Conrad and Aunt Ginny millionaires?

JIMMIE

No.

THE WOLF

Well, your Uncle Marsellus is. And I'm positive if Uncle Conrad and Aunt Ginny were millionaires, they would've furnished you with a whole bedroom set, which your Uncle Marsellus is more than happy to do.

(takes out a roll of bills)

I like oak myself, that's what's in my bedroom. How 'bout you Jimmie, you an oak man?

JIMMIE

Oak's nice.

84. INT. GARAGE – MORNING 84.

Both Jules and Vincent are inside the car cleaning it up. Vincent is in the front seat washing windows, while Jules is in the backseat, picking up little pieces of skull and gobs of brain. Both are twice as bloody as they were before.

JULES
I will never forgive your ass for this shit. This is some fucked-up repugnant shit!

VINCENT
Did you ever hear the philosophy that once a man admits he's wrong, he's immediately forgiven for all wrong-doings?

JULES
Man, get outta my face with that shit! The motherfucker who said that never had to pick up itty-bitty pieces of skull with his fingers on account of your dumb ass.

VINCENT
I got a threshold, Jules. I got a threshold for the abuse I'll take. And you're crossin' it. I'm a race car and you got me in the red. Redline 7000, that's where you are. Just know, it's fuckin' dangerous to be drivin' a race car when it's in the red. It could blow.

JULES
You're gettin' ready to blow? I'm a mushroom-cloud-layin' motherfucker! Every time my fingers touch brain I'm "SUPERFLY T.N.T," I'm the "GUNS OF NAVARONE." I'm what Jimmie Walker usta talk about. In fact, what the fuck am I doin' in the back? You're the motherfucker should be on brain detail. We're tradin'. I'm washin' windows and you're pickin' up this nigger's skull.

85. INT. CHEVY NOVA – MORNING 85.

The interior of the car has been cleaned and lined with bedspreads and quilts. Believe it or not, what looked like a portable slaughterhouse can actually pass for a nondescript vehicle.

The Wolf circles the car examining it.

Jules and Vincent stand aside, their clothes are literally a bloody mess, but they do have a sense of pride in what a good job they've done.

THE WOLF
Fine job, gentlemen. We may get out of this yet.

JIMMIE
I can't believe that's the same car.

THE WOLF
Well, let's not start suckin' each other's dicks quite yet. Phase one is complete, clean the car, which moves us right along to phase two, clean you two.

86. EXT. JIMMIE'S BACKYARD – MORNING 86.

Jules and Vincent stand side by side in their black suits, covered in blood, in Jimmie's backyard. Jimmie holds a plastic Hefty trash bag, while The Wolf holds a garden hose with one of those gun nozzles attached.

THE WOLF
Strip.

VINCENT
All the way?

THE WOLF
To your bare ass.

As they follow directions, The Wolf enjoys a smoke.

THE WOLF
Quickly gentlemen, we got about fifteen minutes before Jimmie's better-half comes pulling into the driveway.

JULES
This morning air is some chilly shit.

VINCENT
Are you sure this is absolutely necessary?

THE WOLF
You know what you two look like?

VINCENT
What?

THE WOLF
Like a coupla guys who just blew off somebody's head. Yes, strippin' off those bloody rags is absolutely necessary. Toss the clothes in Jim's garbage bag.

JULES
Now Jimmie, don't do nothin' stupid like puttin' that out in front of your house for Elmo the garbage man to take away.

THE WOLF
Don't worry, we're takin' it with us. Jim, the soap.

He hands the now-naked men a bar of soap.

THE WOLF
Okay gentlemen, you've both been to County before, I'm sure. Here it comes.

He hits the trigger, water SHOOTS OUT, SMACKING both men.

JULES
Goddamn, that water's fuckin' cold!

THE WOLF
Better you than me, gentlemen.

The two men, trembling, scrub themselves.

THE WOLF
Don't be afraid of the soap, spread it around.

The Wolf stops the hose, tossing it on the ground.

THE WOLF
Towel 'em.

Jimmie tosses them each a towel, which they rub furiously across their bodies.

THE WOLF
You're dry enough, give 'em their clothes.

JIMMIE
Okay fellas, in the one-size-fits-all category, we got swim trunks, one red -- one white. And two extra-large tee-shirts. A UC Santa Cruz shirt and an "I'm with Stupid" shirt.

JULES
I get the "I'm with Stupid" shirt.

FADE UP ON:

87. JULES AND VINCENT 87.

in their tee-shirts and swim trunks. They look a million miles away from the black-suited, bad-asses we first met.

THE WOLF
Perfect. Perfect. We couldn't've planned this better. You guys look like...what do they look like, Jimmie?

JIMMIE
Dorks. They look like a couple of dorks.

The Wolf and Jimmie laugh.

JULES
Ha ha ha. They're your clothes, motherfucker.

JIMMIE
I guess you just gotta know how to wear them.

JULES
Yeah, well, our asses ain't the expert on wearin' dorky shit that yours is.

THE WOLF
C'mon, gentlemen, we're laughin' and jokin' our way into prison. Don't make me beg.

They start walking through the house to the garage.

JIMMIE
Wait a minute, before you guys split, I wanna get a picture of this.

JULES
Jimmie, have you forgotten about your wife comin' home?

JIMMIE
It won't take a second.

VINCENT
I don't like this photograph shit.

JIMMIE
Sorry -- my house, my rules.

88. INT. JIMMIE'S GARAGE – MORNING 88.

The garbage bag is tossed in the car trunk on top of Marvin. The Wolf SLAMS it closed.

THE WOLF
Gentlemen, let's get our rules of the road straight. We're going to a place called Monster Joe's Truck and Tow. Monster Joe and his daughter Raquel are sympathetic to our dilemma. The place is North Hollywood, so a few twist and turns aside, we'll be goin' up Hollywood Way. Now I'll drive the tainted car. Jules, you ride with me. Vincent, you follow in my Porsche. Now if we cross the path of any John Q. Laws, nobody does a fuckin' thing 'til I do something.
(to Jules)
What did I say?

JULES
Don't do shit unless --

THE WOLF
-- unless what?

JULES
Unless you do it first.

THE WOLF
Spoken like a true prodigy.
(to Vincent)
How 'bout you, Lash Larue? Can you keep your spurs from jingling and jangling?

VINCENT
I'm cool, Mr. Wolf. My gun just went off, I dunno how.

THE WOLF
Fair enough.
(he throws Vince his car keys)
I drive real fuckin' fast, so keep up. If I get my car back any different than I gave it, Monster Joe's gonna be disposing of two bodies.

JULES
Why do you drive fast?

THE WOLF
Because it's a lot of fun.

Jules and Vincent laugh.

THE WOLF
Let's move.

Jimmie comes through the door, camera in hand.

JIMMIE
Wait a minute, I wanna take a picture.

JULES
We ain't got time, man.

JIMMIE
We got time for one picture. You and Vincent get together.

Jules and Vincent stand next to each other.

JIMMIE
Okay, you guys put your arms around each other.

The two men look at each other and, after a long beat, a smile breaks out. They put their arms around each other.

JIMMIE
Okay Winston, get in there.

THE WOLF
I ain't no model.

JIMMIE
After what a cool guy I've been, I can't believe you do me like this. It's the only thing I asked.

JULES & VINCENT
C'mon, Mr. Wolf....

THE WOLF
Okay, one photo and we go.

SLOW DOLLY TOWARD A LONE CAMERA.

JIMMIE (OS)
Everybody say Pepsi.

JULES (OS)
I ain't fuckin' sayin' Pepsi.

JIMMIE (OS)
Smile, Winston.

THE WOLF
I don't smile in pictures.

The camera goes off, FLASHING THE SCREEN WHITE.

THE PHOTO FADES UP OVER WHITE:
it's Jules and Vincent, their arms around each other, next to Jimmie, whose arm is around The Wolf. Everyone is smiling except you-know-who.

89. INT. MONSTER JOE'S TRUCK AND TOW – MORNING 89.

Winston is counting out three thousand dollars to an older man in a dirty tee-shirt, MONSTER JOE. We're in Joe's office, which looks like the office of every tow yard on the planet. A filthy, disarrayed mess.

MONSTER JOE
I've said it before, I'll say it again, your business is always welcome.

WINSTON
I would think by now I've earned the equivalent of Frequent Flyer miles.

MONSTER JOE
I'll tell ya what, if you ever need it, I'll dispose of a body part for free.

WINSTON
How 'bout an upgrade, you dispose a whole body for the price of a body part.

The two men laugh.

MONSTER JOE
That one I need to speak with my accountant on.

WINSTON
Where's that reprobate daughter of yours?

MONSTER JOE
Out in the yard, up to no good.

90. EXT. MONSTER JOE'S TRUCK AND TOW – MORNING 90.

Winston steps outside and is joined by Monster Joe's daughter, RAQUEL. They walk in step across the yard with their arms around each other's waists.

RAQUEL
Hello, Boyfriend!

WINSTON
Hello, Girlfriend. I swear, heartbreaker, Joe should change the name of this place to Beauty and the Beast Truck and Tow.

RAQUEL
You're prejudiced because you love me.

WINSTON
Guilty.

RAQUEL
Now business is done, it's time for pleasure.

WINSTON
The time it is, is time for bed.

RAQUEL
Contre senior Lobo.

WINSTON
Do you have a different idea?

RAQUEL
Most definitely.

WINSTON
What do you think?

RAQUEL
I think you're taking me out to breakfast.

WINSTON
Well, you thought wrong.

RAQUEL
That's no fair! I never get to see you.

WINSTON
Raquel, I been up all night. I need sleep. You understand the concept of sleep?

RAQUEL
Yes, sleep is what you do after you've taken me to breakfast. Just get used to the idea, indulging me is the price of doing business at Monster Joe's Truck and Tow.

WINSTON
Raquel --

RAQUEL
I haven't seen you in a long time. I miss you, we're going to breakfast. So it is written, so shall it be done.

They exit the tow yard. Jules and Vincent wait by Winston's Porsche.

JULES
We cool?

WINSTON
Like it never happened.

Jules and Vincent bump fists.

JULES
I apologize for bein' in your shit like I was.

VINCENT
You had every right, I fucked up.

RAQUEL
(to Winston)
Are they having a moment?

WINSTON
Boys, this is Raquel. Someday, all this will be hers.

RAQUEL
(to the boys)
Hi. You know, if they ever do "I SPY: THE MOTION PICTURE," you guys, I'd be great. What's with the outfits. You guys going to a volleyball game?

Winston laughs, the boys groan.

WINSTON
I'm takin' m'lady out to breakfast. Maybe I can drop you two off. Where do you live?

VINCENT
Redondo Beach.

JULES
Inglewood.

Winston grabs Jules' wrist and pantomimes like he's in a "DEAD ZONE" trance.

WINSTON
(painfully)
It's your future: I see...a cab ride.
(dropping the act)
Sorry guys, move out of the sticks.
(to Raquel)
Say goodbye, Raquel.

RAQUEL
Goodbye, Raquel.

WINSTON
I'll see you two around, and stay outta trouble, you crazy kids.

Winston turns to leave.

JULES
Mr. Wolf.

He turns around.

JULES
It was a pleasure watchin' you work.

The Wolf smiles.

WINSTON
Call me Winston.

He turns and banters with Raquel as they get in the Porsche.

WINSTON
You hear that, young lady? Respect. You could learn a lot from those two fine specimens. Respect for one's elders shows character.

RAQUEL
I have character.

WINSTON
Just because you are a character doesn't mean you have character.

RAQUEL
Oh you're so funny, oh you're so funny.

The Porsche SHOOTS OFF down the road.

The two men left alone look at each other.

JULES
Wanna share a cab?

VINCENT
You know I could go for some breakfast. Want to have breakfast with me?

JULES
Sure.

91. INT. COFFEE SHOP — MORNING 91.

Jules and Vincent sit at a booth. In front of Vincent is a big stack of pancakes and sausages, which he eats with gusto.

Jules, on the other hand, just has a cup of coffee and a muffin. He seems far away in thought. The Waitress pours a refill for both men.

VINCENT
Thanks a bunch.
(to Jules, who's nursing his coffee)
Want a sausage?

JULES
Naw, I don't eat pork.

VINCENT
Are you Jewish?

JULES
I ain't Jewish man, I just don't dig on swine.

VINCENT
Why not?

JULES
They're filthy animals. I don't eat filthy animals.

VINCENT
Sausages taste good. Pork chops taste good.

JULES
A sewer rat may taste like pumpkin pie. I'll never know 'cause even if it did, I wouldn't eat the filthy motherfucker. Pigs sleep and root in shit. That's a filthy animal. I don't wanna eat nothin' that ain't got enough sense to disregard its own feces.

VINCENT
How about dogs? Dogs eat their own feces.

JULES
I don't eat dog either.

VINCENT
Yes, but do you consider a dog to be a filthy animal?

JULES
I wouldn't go so far as to call a dog filthy, but they're definitely dirty. But a dog's got personality. And personality goes a long way.

VINCENT
So by that rationale, if a pig had a better personality, he'd cease to be a filthy animal?

JULES
We'd have to be talkin' 'bout one motherfuckin' charmin' pig. It'd have to be the Cary Grant of pigs.

The two men laugh.

VINCENT
Good for you. Lighten up a little. You been sittin' there all quiet.

JULES
I just been sittin' here thinkin'.

VINCENT
(mouthful of food)
About what?

JULES
The miracle we witnessed.

VINCENT
The miracle _you_ witnessed. _I_ witnessed a freak occurrence.

JULES
Do you know what a miracle is?

VINCENT
An act of God.

JULES
What's an act of God?

VINCENT
I guess it's when God makes the impossible possible. And I'm sorry Jules, but I don't think what happened this morning qualifies.

JULES

Don't you see, Vince, that shit don't matter. You're judging this thing the wrong way. It's not about what. It could be God stopped the bullets, he changed Coke into Pepsi, he found my fuckin' car keys. You don't judge shit like this based on merit. Whether or not what we experienced was an according-to-Hoyle miracle is insignificant. What is significant is I felt God's touch. God got involved.

VINCENT

But why?

JULES

That's what's fuckin' wit' me! I don't know why. But I can't go back to sleep.

VINCENT

So you're serious, you're really gonna quit?

JULES

The life, most definitely.

Vincent takes a bite of food. Jules takes a sip of coffee. In the b.g., we see a PATRON call the Waitress.

PATRON

Garcon! Coffee!

We recognize the patron to be Pumpkin from the first scene of Pumpkin and Honey Bunny.

VINCENT

So if you're quitting the life, what'll you do?

JULES

That's what I've been sitting here contemplating. First, I'm gonna deliver this case to Marsellus. Then, basically, I'm gonna walk the earth.

VINCENT

What do you mean, walk the earth?

JULES
You know, like Caine in "KUNG FU." Just walk from town to town, meet people, get in adventures.

VINCENT
How long do you intend to walk the earth?

JULES
Until God puts me where he wants me to be.

VINCENT
What if he never does?

JULES
If it takes forever, I'll wait forever.

VINCENT
So you decided to be a bum?

JULES
I'll just be Jules, Vincent -- no more, no less.

VINCENT
No Jules, you're gonna be like those pieces of shit out there who beg for change. They walk around like a bunch of fuckin' zombies, they sleep in garbage bins, they eat what I throw away, and dogs piss on 'em. They got a word for 'em, they're called bums. And without a job, residence, or legal tender, that's what you're gonna be -- a fuckin' bum!

JULES
Look my friend, this is just where me and you differ --

VINCENT
-- what happened was peculiar -- no doubt about it -- but it wasn't water into wine.

JULES
All shapes and sizes, Vince.

VINCENT
Stop fuckin' talkin' like that!

JULES
If you find my answers frightening, Vincent, you should cease askin' scary questions.

VINCENT
When did you make this decision -- while you were sitting there eatin' your muffin?

JULES
Yeah. I was just sitting here drinking my coffee, eating my muffin, playin' the incident in my head, when I had what alcoholics refer to as a "moment of clarity."

VINCENT
I gotta take a shit. To be continued.

Vincent exits for the restroom.

Jules, alone, takes a mouthful of muffin, then...Pumpkin and Honey Bunny rise with guns raised.

PUMPKIN
Everybody be cool, this is a robbery!

HONEY BUNNY
Any of you fuckin' pricks move and I'll execute every one of you motherfuckers! Got that?!

Jules looks up, not believing what he's seeing. Under the table, Jules' hand goes to his .45 Automatic. He pulls it out, COCKING IT.

PUMPKIN
Customers stay seated, waitresses on the floor.

HONEY BUNNY
Now means fuckin' now! Do it or die, do it or fucking die!

Like lightning, Pumpkin moves over to the kitchen. While Honey Bunny SCREAMS out threats to the PATRONS, keeping them terrified.

PUMPKIN
You Mexicans in the kitchen, get out here! Hasta luego!

Three COOKS and two BUSBOYS come out of the kitchen.

PUMPKIN
On the floor or I'll cook your ass, comprende?

They comprende. The portly MANAGER speaks up.

MANAGER
I'm the manager here, there's no problem, no problem at all --

Pumpkin heads his way.

PUMPKIN
You're gonna give me a problem?

He reaches him and sticks the barrel of his gun hard in the Manager's neck.

PUMPKIN
What? You said you're gonna give me a problem?

MANAGER
No, I'm not. I'm not gonna give you any problems!

PUMPKIN
I don't know, Honey Bunny. He looks like the hero type to me!

HONEY BUNNY
Don't take any chances. Execute him!

The Patrons SCREAM. Jules watches all this silently, his hand tightly gripping the .45 Automatic under the table.

MANAGER
Please don't! I'm not a hero. I'm just a coffee shop manager. Take anything you want.

PUMPKIN
Tell everybody to cooperate and it'll be all over.

MANAGER
Everybody just be calm and cooperate with them and this will be all over soon!

PUMPKIN
Well done, now git your fuckin' ass on the ground.

92. INT. COFFEE SHOP BATHROOM – MORNING 92.

Vincent, on the toilet, oblivious to the pandemonium outside, reads his "MODESTY BLAISE" book.

93. INT. COFFEE SHOP – MORNING 93.

Cash register drawer opens. Pumpkin stuffs the money from the till in his pocket. Then walks from behind the counter with a trash bag in his hand.

PUMPKIN
Okay people, I'm going to go 'round and collect your wallets. Don't talk, just toss 'em in the bag. We clear?

Pumpkin goes around collecting wallets. Jules sits with his .45 ready to spit under the table.

Pumpkin sees Jules sitting in his booth, holding his wallet, briefcase next to him. Pumpkin crosses to him, his tone more respectful, his manner more on guard.

PUMPKIN
In the bag.

Jules DROPS his wallet in the bag. Using his gun as a pointer, Pumpkin points to the briefcase.

PUMPKIN
What's in that?

JULES
My boss' dirty laundry.

PUMPKIN
Your boss makes you do his laundry?

JULES
When he wants it clean.

PUMPKIN
Sounds like a shit job.

JULES
Funny, I've been thinkin' the same thing.

PUMPKIN
Open it up.

Jules' free hand lays palm flat on the briefcase.

JULES
'Fraid I can't do that.

Pumpkin is definitely surprised by his answer. He aims the gun right in the middle of Jules' face and pulls back the hammer.

PUMPKIN
I didn't hear you.

JULES
Yes, you did.

This exchange has been kind of quiet, not everybody heard it, but Honey Bunny senses something's wrong.

HONEY BUNNY
What's goin' on?

PUMPKIN
Looks like we got a vigilante in our midst.

HONEY BUNNY
Shoot 'em in the face!

JULES
I don't mean to shatter your ego, but this ain't the first time I've had gun pointed at me.

PUMPKIN
You don't open up that case, it's gonna be the last.

MANAGER
(on the ground)
Quit causing problems, you'll get us all killed! Give 'em what you got and get 'em out of here.

JULES
Keep your fuckin' mouth closed, fat man, this ain't any of your goddamn business!

PUMPKIN
I'm countin' to three, and if your hand ain't off that case, I'm gonna unload right in your fuckin' face. Clear? One...

Jules closes his eyes.

PUMPKIN
...two...

Jules SHOOTS Pumpkin twice, up through the table, sending him to the floor. While still in the booth, he SWINGS around to Honey Bunny, who has aimed at Jules, but slowed down by the shock of Pumpkin getting shot. He FIRES three times.

Honey Bunny takes all three HITS in the chest. As she FALLS SCREAMING, she FIRES wildly, HITTING a SURFER PATRON.

SURFER
She shot me! I'm dying! Sally! Sally!

Jules now brings the gun down to Pumpkin's face. Pumpkin lies shot on the floor at Jules' feet. Pumpkin looks up at the big gun.

JULES
Wrong guy, Ringo.

Jules FIRES straight at the CAMERA, BLINDING US with his FLASH.

Jules' eyes, still closed, suddenly open.

Pumpkin still stands, holding the gun on him.

PUMPKIN
...three.

JULES
You win.

Jules raises his hand off the briefcase.

JULES
It's all yours, Ringo.

PUMPKIN
Open it.

Jules flips the locks and opens the case, revealing it to Pumpkin but not to us. The same light SHINES from the case. Pumpkin's expression goes to amazement. Honey Bunny, across the room, can't see shit.

HONEY BUNNY
What is it? What is it?

PUMPKIN
(softly)
Is that what I think it is?

Jules nods his head: "yes."

PUMPKIN
It's beautiful.

Jules nods his head: "yes."

HONEY BUNNY
Goddammit, what is it?

Jules SLAMS the case closed, then sits back, as if offering the case to Pumpkin. Pumpkin, one big smile, bends over to pick up the case.

Like a rattlesnake, Jules' free hand GRABS the wrist of Pumpkin's gun hand, SLAMMING it on the table. His other hand comes from under the table and STICKS the barrel of his .45 hard under Pumpkin's chin.

Honey Bunny freaks out, waving her gun in Jules' direction.

HONEY BUNNY
Let him go! Let him go! I'll blow your fuckin' head off! I'll kill ya! I'll kill ya! You're gonna die, you're gonna fuckin' die bad!

JULES
(to Pumpkin)
Tell that bitch to be cool! Say, bitch be cool! Say, bitch be cool!

PUMPKIN
Chill out, honey!

HONEY BUNNY
Let him go!

JULES
(softly)
Tell her it's gonna be okay.

PUMPKIN
It's gonna be okay.

JULES
Promise her.

PUMPKIN
I promise.

JULES
Tell her to chill.

PUMPKIN
Just chill out.

JULES
What's her name?

PUMPKIN
Yolanda.

Whenever Jules talks to Yolanda, he never looks at her, only at Pumpkin.

JULES
(to Yolanda)
So, we cool Yolanda? We ain't gonna do anything stupid, are we?

YOLANDA
(crying)
Don't you hurt him.

JULES
Nobody's gonna hurt anybody. We're gonna be like three Fonzies. And what's Fonzie like?

No answer.

JULES
C'mon Yolanda, what's Fonzie like?

YOLANDA
(through tears, unsure)
He's cool?

JULES
Correct-amundo! And that's what we're gonna be, we're gonna be cool.
(to Pumpkin)
Now Ringo, I'm gonna count to three and I want you to let go your gun and lay your palms flat on the table. But when you do it, do it cool. Ready?

Pumpkin looks at him.

JULES
One...two...three.

Pumpkin lets go of his gun and places both hands on the table. Yolanda can't stand it anymore.

YOLANDA
Okay, now let him go!

JULES
Yolanda, I thought you were gonna be cool. When you yell at me, it makes me nervous. When I get nervous, I get scared. And when motherfuckers get scared, that's when motherfuckers get accidentally shot.

YOLANDA
(more conversational)
Just know: you hurt him, you die.

JULES
That seems to be the situation. Now I don't want that and you don't want that and Ringo here don't want that. So let's see what we can do.
(to Ringo)
Now this is the situation. Normally both of your asses would be dead as fuckin' fried chicken. But you happened to pull this shit while I'm in a transitional period. I don't wanna kill ya, I want to help ya. But I'm afraid I can't give you the case. It don't belong to me. Besides, I went through too much shit this morning on account of this case to just hand it over to your ass.

VINCENT (OS)
What the fuck's goin' on here?

Yolanda WHIPS her gun toward the stranger.

VINCENT, by the bathroom, has his gun out, dead-aimed at Yolanda.

JULES
It's cool, Vincent! It's cool! Don't do a goddamn thing. Yolanda, it's cool baby, nothin's changed. We're still just talkin'.
(to Pumpkin)
Tell her we're still cool.

PUMPKIN
It's cool, Honey Bunny, we're still cool.

VINCENT
(gun raised)
What the hell's goin' on, Jules?

JULES
Nothin' I can't handle. I want you to just hang back and don't do shit unless it's absolutely necessary.

VINCENT
Check.

JULES
Yolanda, how we doin, baby?

YOLANDA
I gotta go pee! I want to go home.

JULES
Just hang in there, baby, you're doing' great. Ringo's proud of you and so am I. It's almost over.
(to Pumpkin)
Now I want you to go in that bag and find my wallet.

PUMPKIN
Which one is it?

JULES
It's the one that says Bad Motherfucker on it.

Pumpkin looks in the bag and -- sure enough -- there's a wallet with "Bad Motherfucker" embroidered on it.

JULES
That's my bad motherfucker. Now open it up and take out the cash. How much is there?

PUMPKIN
About fifteen hundred dollars.

JULES
Put it in your pocket, it's yours. Now with the rest of them wallets and the register, that makes this a pretty successful little score.

VINCENT
Jules, if you give this nimrod fifteen hundred bucks, I'm gonna shoot 'em on general principle.

JULES
You ain't gonna do a goddamn thing, now hang back and shut the fuck up. Besides, I ain't givin' it to him. I'm buyin' somethin' for my money. Wanna know what I'm buyin' Ringo?

PUMPKIN
What?

JULES
Your life. I'm givin' you that money so I don't hafta kill your ass. You read the Bible?

PUMPKIN
Not regularly.

JULES
There's a passage I got memorized. Ezekiel 25:17. "The path of the righteous man is beset on all sides by the inequities of the selfish and the tyranny of evil men. Blessed is he who, in the name of charity and good will, shepherds the weak through the valley of the darkness. For he is truly his brother's keeper and the finder of lost children.
(MORE)

JULES (CONT'D)
And I will strike down upon thee with great vengeance and furious anger those who attempt to poison and destroy my brothers. And you will know I am the Lord when I lay my vengeance upon you." I been sayin' that shit for years. And if you ever heard it, it meant your ass. I never really questioned what it meant. I thought it was just a cold-blooded thing to say to a motherfucker 'fore you popped a cap in his ass. But I saw some shit this mornin' made me think twice. Now I'm thinkin', it could mean you're the evil man. And I'm the righteous man. And Mr. .45 here, he's the shepherd protecting my righteous ass in the valley of darkness. Or it could be you're the righteous man and I'm the shepherd and it's the world that's evil and selfish. I'd like that. But that shit ain't the truth. The truth is you're the weak. And I'm the tyranny of evil men. But I'm tryin'. I'm tryin' real hard to be a shepherd.

Jules lowers his gun, lying it on the table.

Pumpkin looks at him, to the money in his hand, then to Yolanda. She looks back.

Grabbing the trash bag full of wallets, the two RUN out the door.

Jules, who has never risen from his seat the whole time, takes a sip of coffee.

JULES
(to himself)
It's cold.

He pushes it aside.

Vincent appears next to Jules.

VINCENT
I think we oughta leave now.

JULES
That's probably a good idea.

Vincent throws some money on the table and Jules grabs the briefcase.

Then, to the amazement of the Patrons, the Waitresses, the Cooks, the Bus Boys, and the Manager, these two bad-ass dudes -- wearing UC Santa Cruz and "I'm with Stupid" tee-shirts, swim trunks, thongs and packing .45 Automatics -- walk out of the coffee shop together without saying a word.

THE END

Cast

John Travolta	Vincent Vega
Samuel L. Jackson	Jules
Uma Thurman	Mia
Harvey Keitel	The Wolf
Tim Roth	Pumpkin
Amanda Plummer	Honey Bunny
Maria de Medeiros	Fabienne
Ving Rhames	Marsellus Wallace
Eric Stoltz	Lance
Rosanna Arquette	Jody
Christopher Walken	Koons
Bruce Willis	Butch

Crew

Writer/Director	Quentin Tarantino
Producer	Lawrence Bender
Stories by	Quentin Tarantino/Roger Avary
Executive Producer	Danny DeVito
Executive Producer	Michael Shamberg
Executive Producer	Stacey Sher
Co-executive Producer	Bob Weinstein
Co-executive Producer	Harvey Weinstein
Co-executive Producer	Richard N. Gladstein
Director of Photography	Andrzej Sekula
Editor	Sally Menke
Production Designer	David Wasco
Costume Designer	Betsy Heimann
Music Supervisor	Karyn Rachtman
Casting by	Ronnie Yeskel, C.S.A./ Gary M. Zuckerbrod, C.S.A.

About the Author

Quentin Tarantino, both writer and director of *Pulp Fiction,* also plays a role as Jules's high-strung friend, Jimmy, in the film. He burst onto the film scene with his critically acclaimed and controversial debut film *Reservoir Dogs,* the gritty story of six thieves and a jewel heist gone awry. A recent graduate from the prestigious Sundance Institute Director's Workshop and Lab, Tarantino began his career as an actor. After five years of acting, appearing on select television series, he turned his attention to writing screenplays.

While supporting himself by working in a video rental store in Southern California, he wrote the screenplay, *True Romance,* directed by Tony Scott, for which Tarantino has received accolades from the critics.